Some of the Kinder Planets

Tim Wynne-Jones

SOME
OF THE
KINDER
PLANETS

A Groundwood Book
Douglas & McIntyre
Toronto/Vancouver/Buffalo

A shorter version of "The Night of the Pomegranate"
appeared in *Owl Magazine*, Vol. 16, No. 5, May, 1991.

Groundwood Books
Douglas & McIntyre Ltd.
585 Bloor Street West
Toronto, Ontario M6G 1K5

The publisher gratefully acknowledges the assistance of
the Ontario Arts Council and the Canada Council.

Canadian Cataloguing in Publication Data

Wynne-Jones, Tim
    Some of the kinder planets

"A Groundwood book"
ISBN 0-88899-207-6 (mass market pbk.)

I. Title.

PS8595.Y59S6   1993   jC813'.54   C93-094902-1
PZ7.W95So   1993

Design by Michael Solomon
Cover illustration by Alina Gavrielatos
Printed and bound in Canada

For Marg and Klaus Gruber—
two of the kinder people you
could ever hope to meet.

ACKNOWLEDGEMENTS

A crow likes to steal shiny bits of the world and hoard them away in its nest. Pull-tabs, gum wrappers, bread-ties, rings. Writers are like crows. They call their nests stories. I would like to thank all the people from whom I have stolen stuff to make the stories in this collection, but, unfortunately, I can't remember them all. So this list of acknowledgements is only partial. It also includes the names of a few brave souls who have clambered up my tree to comment on how the nest was doing, whether maybe it needed another gum wrapper or so. Thanks, everyone: Peter Carver, Aaron Nault, Michael Nault, Mark Gryski, Sarah Ellis, Rachel Sinn, Janet Lunn, John Lianga, Shelley Tanaka, Jim King, Harry MacKay, Sheila Wynne-Jones, Denise Baker and Jean-Pierre Chrestien of the Museum of Civilization.

I also want to thank Xan, Maddy, Lewis and Amanda, who are a constant source of shiny story-building material.

CONTENTS

THE NIGHT
OF THE
POMEGRANATE

H ARRIET'S solar system was a mess. She had
made it—the sun and its nine planets—out
of rolled-up balls of the morning newspaper. It was
mounted on a sheet of green bristol board. The
bristol board had a project about Austria on the
other side. Harriet wished the background were
black. Green was all wrong.

Everything about her project was wrong. The
crumpled paper was coming undone. Because she
had used the last of the Scotch tape on Saturn's
rings, the three remaining planets had nothing to
keep them scrunched up. Tiny Pluto was already
bigger than Jupiter and growing by the minute. She
had also run out of glue, so part of her solar system
was stuck together with grape chewing gum.

Harriet's big brother, Tom, was annoyed at her
because Mom made him drive her to school early
with her stupid project. Dad was annoyed at her
for using part of the business section. Mostly she
had stuck to the want ads, but then an advertise-
ment printed in red ink in the business section
caught her eye, and she just had to have it for Mars.

Harriet had a crush on Mars; that's what Tom said. She didn't even mind him saying it.

Mars was near the Earth this month. The nights had been November cold but clear as glass, and Harriet had been out to see Mars every night, which was why she hadn't got her solar system finished, why she was so tired, why Mom made Tom drive her to school. It was all Mars's fault.

———

She was using the tape on Ms. Krensky's desk when Clayton Beemer arrived with his dad. His solar system came from the hobby store. The planets were Styrofoam balls, all different sizes and painted the right colours. Saturn's rings were clear plastic painted over as delicately as insect wings.

Harriet looked at her own Saturn. Her rings were drooping despite all the tape. They looked like a limp skirt on a . . . on a ball of scrunched-up newspaper.

Harriet sighed. The wires that supported Clayton's planets in their black box were almost invisible. The planets seemed to float.

"What d'ya think?" Clayton asked. He beamed. Mr. Beemer beamed. Harriet guessed that *he* had made the black box with its glittery smears of stars.

She had rolled up her own project protectively when Clayton entered the classroom. Suddenly one of the planets came unstuck and fell on the floor. Clayton and Mr. Beemer looked at it.

"What's that?" asked Clayton.

"Pluto, I think," said Harriet, picking it up. She popped it in her mouth. It tasted of grape gum.

"Yes, Pluto," she said. Clayton and Mr. Beemer walked away to find the best place to show off their project.

Darjit arrived next. "Hi, Harriet," she said. The project under her arm had the planets' names done in bold gold lettering. Harriet's heart sank. Pluto tasted stale and cold.

———

But last night Harriet had tasted pomegranates. Old Mrs. Pond had given her one while she busied herself putting on layer after layer of warm clothing and gathering the things they would need for their Mars watch.

Mrs. Pond lived in the country. She lived on the edge of the woods by a meadow that sloped down to a marsh through rough frost-licked grass and prickly ash and juniper. It was so much darker than town; good for star-gazing.

By eleven P.M. Mars was directly above the marsh, which was where Harriet and Mrs. Pond set themselves up for their vigil. They found it just where they had left it the night before: in the constellation Taurus between the Pleiades and the Hyades. But you didn't need a map to find Mars these nights. It shone like rust, neither trembling nor twinkling as the fragile stars did.

Mrs. Pond smiled and handed Harriet two folded-up golfers' chairs. "Ready?" she asked.

———

"Ready, class?" said Ms. Krensky. Everyone took their seats. Harriet placed the green bristol board universe in front of her. It was an even worse mess than it had been when she arrived. Her solar system was ravaged.

It had started off with Pluto and then, as a joke to make Darjit laugh, she had eaten Neptune. Then Karen had come in, and Jodi and Nick and Scott.

"The planet taste test," Harriet had said, ripping off a bit of Mercury. "Umm, very spicy." By the time the bell rang there wasn't much of her project left.

Kevin started. He stood at the back of the classroom holding a green and blue marble.

"If this was Earth," he said, "then the sun would be this big —" He put the Earth in his pocket and then pulled a fat squishy yellow beachball from a garbage bag. Everybody hooted and clapped. "And it would be at the crosswalk," he added. Everyone looked confused, so Ms. Krensky helped Kevin explain the relative distances between the Earth and the sun. "And Pluto would be eighty kilometres away from here," said Kevin. But then he wasn't sure about that, so Ms. Krensky worked it out at the board with him.

Meanwhile, using Kevin's example, the class was supposed to figure out where other planets in the solar system would be relative to the green and blue marble in Kevin's pocket. Harriet sighed.

Until last night, Harriet had never seen the inside of a pomegranate before. As she opened the hard rind, she marvelled at the bright red seeds in their cream-coloured fleshy pouches.

"It's like a little secret universe all folded in on itself," said Mrs. Pond.

Harriet tasted it. With her tongue, she popped a little red bud against the roof of her mouth. The taste startled her, made her laugh.

"Tonight," Mrs. Pond said, "Mars is only 77 million kilometres away." They drank a cocoa toast to that. Then she told Harriet about another time when Mars had been even closer on its orbit around the sun. She had been a girl then, and had heard on the radio the famous broadcast of "The War of the Worlds." An actor named Orson Welles had made a radio drama based on a story about Martians attacking the world, but he had made it in a series of news bulletins and reports, and a lot of people had believed it was true.

Harriet listened to Mrs. Pond and sipped her cocoa and stared at the Earth's closest neighbour and felt deliciously chilly and warm at the same time. Mars was wonderfully clear in the telescope, but even with the naked eye she could imagine canals and raging storms. She knew there weren't really Martians, but she allowed herself to imagine them anyway. She imagined one of them preparing for his invasion of the Earth, packing his laser gun, a thermos of cocoa and a golfer's chair.

"What in heaven's name is this?" Ms. Krensky was standing at Harriet's chair staring down at the green bristol board. There was only one planet left.

"Harriet says it's Mars." Darjit started giggling.

"And how big is Mars?" asked Ms. Krensky. Her eyes said Unsatisfactory.

"Compared to Kevin's marble earth, Mars would be the size of a pomegranate seed, including the juicy red pulp," said Harriet. Ms. Krensky walked to the front of the class. She turned at her desk. Was there the hint of a smile on her face?

"And where is it?" she asked, raising an eyebrow.

Harriet looked at the calculations she had done on a corner of the green bristol board. "If the sun was at the crosswalk," said Harriet, "then Mars would be much closer. Over there." She pointed out the window at the slide in the kindergarten playground. Some of the class actually looked out the window to see if they could see it.

"You *can* see Mars," said Harriet. "Sometimes." Now she was sure she saw Ms. Krensky smile.

"How many of you have seen Mars?" the teacher asked. Only Harriet and Randy Pilcher put up their hands. But Randy had only seen it on the movie *Total Recall*.

"Last night was a special night, I believe," said Ms. Krensky, crossing her arms and leaning against her desk. Harriet nodded. "Tell us about it, Harriet," said the teacher.

So Harriet did. She told them all about Mrs. Pond and the Mars watch. She started with the pomegranate.

SAVE THE MOON
FOR KERDY DICKUS

This is Ky's story. It happened to her. It happened at her place in the country. I wasn't there when it happened, but I know what her place in the country looks like, and that's important. In this story, the way things look is really important.

There's more than one version of this story. If Ky's younger brothers, Brad or Tony, told you the story, it would come out different. But not as different as the way the Stranger tells it. We know his name now, but we still call him the Stranger. Perhaps you know his version of the story. It was in the newspapers. Well, the *National Enquirer*, anyway.

———

Ky's father, Tan Mori, built their house in the country. It's a dome. It looks like a glass igloo, but it's actually made of a web of light metal tubing and a special clear plastic. From the outside you can see right into the house, which Ky didn't like one bit at first, because it wasn't very private. But the house is at the end of a long driveway surrounded by woods, so the only things that can look at you are bluejays, raccoons, the occasional deer and, from way up high on a hot day, turkey vultures circling the sky.

It wasn't a hot day when this story happened. It was two days before Christmas and there was a bad freezing rain. But let me tell you more about the house, because you have to be able to see the house in order to understand what happened. You have to imagine it the way the Stranger saw it.

For one thing there's all this high-tech office stuff. Ky's parents are both computer software designers, which means that just about everything they do can be done on a computer. Word processors, video monitors, a modem, a fax machine — they're always popping on and off. Their lights blink in the dark.

You also have to know something about Ky's family if you want to see what the Stranger saw when he arrived at their door. You especially have to know that they have family traditions. They make them up all the time. For instance, for the past three years it's been a tradition that I go up from the city for Ky's birthday in the summer, and we go horseback riding. I'm not sure if that's what tradition really means, but it's nice.

It's also a tradition with Ky's family to watch the movie *It's a Wonderful Life* every Christmas. And so, two nights before Christmas, that's what they were doing. They were wearing their traditional Christmastime nightclothes. They were all in red: red flannel pyjamas, even red slippers. Ky had her hair tied back in a red scrunchie. That's what the Stranger saw: this family in red.

They had just stopped the movie for a break. They were going to have okonomiyaki, which is kind of like a Japanese pizza and pancake all mixed up together with shredded cabbage and crabmeat and this chewy wheat gluten stuff called seitan. This is a tradition, too. Ky's father, Tan, likes to cook. So they watch *It's a Wonderful Life* and they have this mid-movie snack served with kinpara gobo, which is spicy, and other pickly things that only Tan and Barbara, Ky's mother, bother to eat. But the kids like okonomiyaki.

Tan Mori is Japanese. Here's how he looks. He wears clear rimmed glasses. He's short and trim and has long black hair that he wears pulled tightly back in a ponytail.

Ky doesn't think the Stranger had ever seen a Japanese person up close before. He probably hadn't ever seen someone who looked like Barbara Mori, either. She isn't Japanese. She has silvery blonde hair but it's cut very, very short so that you can see the shape of her head. She's very slim, bony, and she has one of the nicest smiles you could imagine. She has two dark spots beside her mouth. Ky calls them beauty marks; Barbara laughs and calls them moles.

It was Barbara who first noticed the Stranger while Tan was cooking the okonomiyaki and the boys were getting bowls of shrimp chips and Coke and Ky was boiling water for green tea.

The freezing rain was pouring down on the dome, but inside it was warm, and there were little islands of light. A single light on a post lit up the driveway a bit.

"There's someone out there," said Barbara. "The poor man." She went to the door and called to him. The kids left what they were doing to go and look.

He was big and shadowy where he was standing. He was also stoop-shouldered, trying to hide his head from the icy downpour.

Barbara waved at him. "Come!" she called as loudly as she could. "Come." Her teeth were chattering because she was standing at the open door in her pyjamas and cold wind was pouring in.

The Stranger paused. He seemed uncertain. Then a gust of wind made him lose his balance and he slipped on the ice and fell. When he got up he made his way towards the house slowly, sliding and slipping the whole long way. He was soaked clear through all over. He only had a jean jacket on. No gloves or hat. As he approached the house, Ky could see that, although he was big, he was young, a teenager. Then Barbara sent her to the bathroom for a big towel.

By the time she got back with the towel, the boy was in the house, standing there dripping in the hall. Barbara wrapped the towel around his shoulders. She had to stand on her toes; he was big. He had black hair and he reminded Ky of a bear she had seen at the zoo after it had been swimming. He smelled terrible. His wet clothes smelled of alcohol and cigarette smoke. The kids all stepped away from him. Tony crinkled up his nose, but Barbara didn't seem to care.

"Come in and get warm," she said, leading him towards the kitchen.

I haven't told you about the kitchen yet. Well, there is a kind of island shaped like a kidney with a built-in stove and sink. Since the walls of the dome are curved, all the cupboards and drawers and stuff are built into the island. Lights recessed into the ceiling above bathe the island in a warm glow so that the maple countertop looks like a beach.

Tan was already pouring the Stranger some tea when Barbara brought him over and tried to sit him down near the stove where it was warmest. But he wouldn't sit. Tan handed him a tiny cup of steaming tea. The cup had no handle. The Stranger didn't seem to know what to do, but the warmth alone was enough to make him take it. His hands were huge and strong and rough. The tiny cup looked like it would break if he closed his fist.

He took a sip of the tea. His eyes cleared a bit.

"Dad's in the truck," he said.

"Oh, my God," said Barbara. "Where? We should get him. Tan?"

The Stranger nodded his big bear head in the direction that the truck was but, of course, you couldn't see it from the house. Ky looked down the driveway, but there is a bend in it so she couldn't see the road.

Tan had turned off the gas under the frying pans and was heading towards the closet for his coat.

"I'll bring him back," he said.

"No!" said the Stranger. His voice cracked a little. "He's okay. He's sleepin'. Truck's warm."

— 19 —

Nobody in the Mori family knew what to do. Tony looked about ready to laugh. Ky glared at him. Tan shrugged and looked at Barbara. "It's not too cold as long as he's sheltered." She nodded and Tan turned the stove back on. The okonomiyaki were ready to flip. He flipped them. The Stranger stared at them. Maybe he thought they were the weirdest pancakes he'd ever seen. It's hard to know what he was thinking. Then he looked around.

"Where am I?" he asked.

"The fifth line," said Barbara, filling his cup. The Mori house is on the fifth concession line of Leopold County.

"The fifth?" he asked. He stared around again. He looked as if he didn't believe it. "The fifth?" He stared at Barbara, who nodded. He stared at Tan. Tan nodded, too. The Stranger kept staring at Tan, at his red pyjamas, his long ponytail, his bright dark eyes behind clear rimmed glasses. "Where am I?"

That's when the fax machine started beeping and the Stranger spilled his tea. Brad got him a tea towel but he didn't seem hurt. He stared into the dark where the computer stuff is. There are hardly any walls in the dome.

The fax machine beeps when a transmission is coming through. Then it makes a whirring sound and paper starts rolling out with a message on it.

The boy watched the fax machine blinking in the shadows, because the lights were not on in the office part of the dome.

"It's just what my parents do," said little Tony. The machinery was still a mystery to him, too.

The Stranger looked at Tan again — all around at the dome. There's a second floor loft but it's not big, so the Stranger could see clear up to the curving roof and out at the rain pelting down. If there had been stars out he could have seen them. He seemed to get a little dizzy from looking up.

"Sit," said Barbara, and this time she made him sit on a stool next to the kitchen island. He steadied himself. To Ky he looked like someone who had just woken up and had no idea what was going on.

By now the fax machine was spewing out a great long roll of paper which curled to the floor. The Stranger watched it for a minute.

"I think we should get your father," said Barbara in a very gentle voice.

"No," said the boy firmly. "He's asleep, eh. We was at Bernie's. You know Bernie?"

But none of the Moris knew Bernie. "Cards," he said. "Having a few drinks ... Christmas ..." He looked back at the fax. "What is this place?"

Tan laughed. He flipped two okonomiyaki onto a warm plate and handed them to the boy. "Here. You look like you could do with something warm to eat."

"More to read?" asked the boy. He thought Tan had said more to read.

Tan handed him the pancakes. "Try it," he said.

Ky went and got the spicy sauce. She poured a bit on the pancake and sprinkled some nori, toasted seaweed, on top. The Stranger looked at Ky and at the food steaming under his nose. It must have smelled funny to him. He looked around again. He was having trouble putting all this together. These strange sweet salty smells, these people all in red.

"You never heard of Bernie?" he asked.

"No," said Ky.

"Bernie Nystrom?"

"Never heard of him."

"Over on the . . ." he was going to say where it was that Bernie Nystrom lived, but he seemed to forget. "Dad's out in the car," he said. "We got lost."

"Not a great night for driving," said Tan, filling the Stranger's cup with more steaming tea.

"Saw your light there," he said, squinting hard as if the light had just shone in his eyes. "Slid right out." He made a sliding gesture with his hand.

"It's pretty icy," said Tan.

"Never seen such a bright light," said the Stranger.

Ky remembers him saying this. It rankled her. He made it sound as if their light had been responsible for his accident. Her mother winked at her.

Tony looked like he was going to say something. Brad put his hand over his brother's mouth. Tony struggled but the Stranger didn't notice. The fax stopped.

"You sure you ain't never heard of Bernie?" he asked one more time. It seemed to matter a great deal, as if he couldn't imagine someone not knowing good ol' Bernie Nystrom.

"Is there someone we could phone for you?" Barbara asked. "Do you need a tow or something?"

The Stranger was staring at the okonomiyaki. "Anita who?" he asked. At that, both Brad and Tony started giggling until Ky shushed them up.

"A *tow* truck," said Barbara, very carefully. "To get you out of the ditch."

The boy put the plate down without touching the food. He rubbed his hands on his wet pants. He was shivering. Barbara sent Brad to get a blanket.

"Could I use your phone?" the boy asked. Ky ran to get the cordless phone from the office area. There was a phone closer, but Ky always uses the cordless.

You have to see this phone to imagine the Stranger's surprise. It's clear plastic. You can see the electronic stuff inside it, the speakers and amplifiers and switches and everything.

The Stranger stared at it, held it up closer to his eyes. That was when Ky thought of all the time travel books she'd read and wondered if this guy was from some other century. Then she remembered that he had come by truck. That's what he'd said, anyway. She wondered if he had been telling the truth. He sure didn't want anyone going to look for his father. Maybe he had been planning on robbing them? But looking at him again, she realized that he was in no condition to rob anyone. She showed him how the phone worked.

"What's your number?" she asked.

"Don't got no number," he said. But he took the phone and slowly punched some numbers anyway. He belched, and a sour smell came from his mouth. Ky stepped back quickly, afraid that he was going to throw up.

The phone rang and rang and no one answered it. Ky watched the Stranger's face. He seemed to fall asleep between each ring and wake up again, not knowing where he was.

"Neighbours," he said, hanging up after about thirty rings. He looked suspiciously at the phone, as if to say, How could I reach anyone I know on a phone like that?

Then he looked at Ky and her family. "Where am I *really*?" he asked.

Brad came back with a comforter and Barbara suggested to the Stranger that he could wear it while she put his wet things in the dryer. He didn't like that idea. But as nice as Barbara is, as small as she is, she can be pretty pushy, and she was afraid he was going to catch pneumonia. So the Stranger found himself without his clothes in a very strange house.

Maybe it was then, to take his mind off wearing only a comforter, that he tried the okonomiyaki. He was very hungry. He wolfed down two helpings, then a third. It was the first time he smiled.

"Hey," said Ky. "It's almost Christmas. You'd better save some room for turkey dinner."

"What?" said the Stranger.

"You'd better save some room for turkey dinner."

The Stranger stopped eating. He stared at the food on his plate. Ky wanted to tell him she was just kidding. She couldn't believe he had taken it so seriously. She was going to say something, but then he asked if he could phone his neighbour again. He still didn't have any luck. But now he seemed real edgy.

Then the telephone answering machine in the office took a long message. It was a computer-expert phoning Tan, and he talked all in computerese, even though it was night time and two days before Christmas.

The Stranger must have heard that voice coming from the dark side of the dome where the lights flashed. Maybe that was what threw him. Or maybe it was when the VCR, which had been on Pause, came back on by itself. Suddenly there were voices from up in the loft. Ky can't remember what part of the movie it was when it came back on. Maybe it was when the angel jumped off the top of the bridge to save the life of the hero. Maybe it was a part like that with dramatic music and lots of shouting and splashing. Maybe the Stranger didn't know it was just a movie on TV. Who knows what he thought was going on there? Maybe in his house there was no TV.

He got edgier and edgier. He started pacing. Then, suddenly, he remembered his neighbour, Lloydy Rintoul.

"You know Lloydy," he said.

Nobody did.

"Sure," he said. "Lloydy Rintoul." He pointed first north and then east and then north again as he tried to get his bearings in this round house with its invisible walls.

"You don't know Lloydy?"

The Stranger, despite his size, suddenly looked like a little lost boy. But then he shook his head and jumped to his feet.

"Lloydy, he's got a tractor," he said. "He'll pull the truck out." He started to leave. "I'll just get him, eh." He forgot he didn't have any clothes on. Tan led him back to his stool. Barbara told him she'd check on the wash. Tan said they should maybe phone Lloydy first. But Lloydy didn't have a phone, either. The people Ky knows in the country all have phones and televisions. But there are people around Leopold County who have lived there longer than anyone and lived poor, scraping out a living on the rocky soil just like their forefathers and foremothers did.

Maybe the kids were looking at the Stranger strangely then, because suddenly he got impatient. Ky said that he looked like a wild bear in a downy comforter cornered by a pack of little people in red pyjamas.

"I'm gonna get Lloydy," he said loudly. It sounded like a threat. It scared the Moris a bit. Barbara decided to get him his clothes even though they were still damp.

And so the Stranger prepared to go. They didn't try to stop him but they insisted that he borrow a big yellow poncho because it was still raining hard.

Now that he had his clothes back on and his escape was imminent, the Stranger calmed down a bit.

"I'll bring it back," he said.

"I'm sure you will," said Tan, as he helped him into the poncho.

Ky went and got him a flashlight, too. It was a silver pencil flashlight she had gotten for her birthday. She had to show him how it worked.

"I'll bring this back," he said to her.

"Okay," she said. "Thanks."

And then he was gone. He slid on the driveway and ended up with a thud on his backside.

"He'll have awful bruises in the morning," said Barbara.

She called to him to come back. She told him she would call for help. He turned halfway down the driveway and seemed to listen, but his hearing wasn't very good even up close, so who knows what he thought she said. She did mention getting the police. Maybe he heard that. Whatever, he turned and ran away, slipping and sliding all the way. Tan considered driving him, but the ice was too treacherous.

"What are the bets," said Brad, "that we never see that stuff again?"

━━━

They never did. The Stranger never did return the poncho or the flashlight. In the morning the family all went out to the road. There was no truck there. Somehow, in his drunken haze, the Stranger must have found Lloydy Rintoul or somebody found him or his dad woke up and got the truck out. It was a mystery.

Ky tried to find Bernie Nystrom's name in the phone book. There was no listing. The boy had never said the name of his neighbour and they already knew that Lloydy Rintoul had no phone, so there was no way of tracking him down. The Moris didn't really care much about getting their stuff back, though. It was Christmas, after all.

———

I saw the story in the *National Enquirer* in January. I was in line at the grocery store with my mother, reading the headlines of the tabloids. I enjoy doing that. There are great stories about tribes in Brazil who look like Elvis Presley, or some seventy-five-year-old woman who gives birth to twin dolphins, or families of eight who live in an abandoned filing cabinet. But this headline jumped off the page at me.

TEEN ABDUCTED BY MARTIANS!

Country boy undergoes torturous experiments while constrained in an alien flying saucer! Experts wonder: Who or what is Kerdy Dickus and what does he want with our moon!

I don't know why I flipped open to page 26 to read the story. I don't know why I paid good money to actually buy the rag. Somehow I knew. And when I showed the picture on page 26 to Ky, she gasped.

It was him. There was the Stranger showing the huge bruises inflicted by the aliens on his arms and ribs and thighs. He told of how he had seen a blinding light and the truck had been pulled right off the road by the saucer's powerful tractor beam. He told of how the aliens had hypnotized him and brought him to their saucer. He told of the drugs they had made him drink; how they had tried to get his father, too, but he had stopped them. He told of the weird food they had made him eat and how it had made him throw up all the next day. His mother could attest to his ill health. "I've never seen him so green," she said. "And he's normally such a healthy lad."

It was his mother who had contacted the *National Enquirer*. She read it all the time and she knew it was a story that would interest them.

His father, too, although he had managed somehow to stay out of the clutches of the aliens' hypnotic powers, could attest to the attack on the car. And then — blackness. There were two hours missing out of his recollection of the night. The aliens had obviously zapped him.

"Something ought to be done about this kind of menace!" said the father.

According to the newspaper, the boy underwent several sessions with a psychiatric investigator after the incident. The investigator specialized in AATT: Alien Abduction Trauma Therapy. He put the boy in a deep trance and interviewed him at length. "Truth drugs" were administered, and all the results concurred: the boy had obviously under-gone a close encounter with alien beings. Under the trance the boy revealed some overheard con-versation that might, the investigator believed, partially explain the purpose of the aliens' trip to earth.

"This might be a recognizance mission." Other experts in the field agreed. "But their long-term goal has to do with our moon and the saving of it. From what? *For* what? It is hard to tell."

One line had become imprinted on the boy's mind. The only spoken part he recalled vividly from his close encounter.

"Save the moon for Kerdy Dickus."

"Perhaps," said the psychiatric investigator, "there is some alien purpose for the boy remembering this one line."

The article went on to give a pretty good account of the aliens, what they looked like, what their flying saucer looked like. But you already know all that.

———

I had heard about the Stranger from Ky. That's how I somehow recognized the story in the *Enquirer*. The next time I saw the Moris, I showed them the paper. But after they had all laughed themselves silly, we talked about it a lot.

Should they try to find the Stranger, now that they knew his name? Even without a phone, they could easily track him down. Should the paper be contacted, so that the truth could be known? What about the psychiatrist who specialized in AATT? The experts?

"I wouldn't mind getting my flashlight back," Ky admitted, but she wasn't really serious.

And so they have never followed up on the story. Ky always imagines she'll run into the Stranger one day in the nearby town. I hope I'm with her. Maybe I'll be up there for her birthday. Maybe it will be raining. Maybe we'll be coming out of a store and he'll be coming in wearing the big yellow poncho. He'll walk right by us, and Ky and I will turn just as he passes and whisper the magic words.

"Save the moon for Kerdy Dickus."

Then we'll hop in our saucer and slip off back to our own world.

THE HOPE BAKERY

WHEN he was only five, Sloane wandered out of the back garden into the woods behind his house. He was gone for some time and everyone got horribly worried, but he arrived home before dark. He didn't understand the greeting he got when he came back out of the woods. Everyone hugged him and kissed him and lectured him between hugs and kisses about not going off like that.

Sloane asked if he was late for supper. He thought that was what all the fuss was about. Of course, nobody had bothered making supper because they were all out looking for him, and so they could only laugh between their tears and say, "No, you're not late for supper." They asked him, "What special thing would you like, sweetheart? Noodles, maybe? Hotdogs?" Sloane wanted mashed potatoes, and everyone agreed that would be very comforting.

But then came the strange part. At dinner he produced a piece of paper from his pocket with the word HOPE on it. The paper was brown; the word was written in pencil.

"Hope?" said his mother.

"It's where I was," he answered.

Mother and Father and Sloane's older sister and brother all looked questioningly at one another and then at Sloane, who was too busy with his mashed potatoes to notice. The thing is, Sloane was only five, and although he knew his letters pretty well, he didn't know too many words. But the writing was unmistakably his. He always put four crossbars on his E's.

"You were at Hope?" his father asked, looking at the wobbly word on the very ragged piece of paper.

"I thought you'd want to know where I was." Sloane stopped eating long enough to extract a stubby pencil from his pocket. "Good I remembered this," he said. "There was paper there, lots of it." He looked around at everyone staring at him. "Don't you know where it is?" he asked. Nobody did.

Sloane said he would take them there. He tried once or twice, but he couldn't find the right path.

So nobody ever learned where Sloane had disappeared to on that scary afternoon when he was only five. The ragged little bit of paper with HOPE written on it stayed on the refrigerator door for a long time beside the shopping lists, the swimming schedules, the Hi & Lois cartoon, the crayon drawings of monsters.

And then on Mother's Day, as a kind of a joke, Father had that piece of brown paper framed in a beautiful wood frame with glass and everything. It was hung on the wall above Mother's desk where the pictures of the kids were. And Sloane, if he ever thought about the adventure, never mentioned it again.

Sloane grew up. When he was seven, another brother came into his life, Todd. So by the time Sloane was twelve, Todd was five.

Sloane found being twelve difficult. Especially school. He was lost at school. He liked lunch and music and geography. He liked maps, liked filling in the sea around continents with a blue pencil crayon. He spent a lot of time at it.

He was upset easily. One morning, waiting for the school bus, Sloane found a dead chipmunk on the front drive and got so broke up about it that he stayed home from school. His older brother, Lawren, teased him about it.

Then one evening, when he was watching television, Sloane saw a lion killing a litter of lion cubs. He wanted to turn off the TV but he wanted to watch it, too. The lion had already driven off the father of the cubs and was taking over the pride, which is what they call a lion family. This new lion didn't want any of the other lion's cubs around. The program didn't actually show the new lion killing anything, but there was a picture of two of the cubs crouching together looking very scared. It was worse than a horror movie. Sloane hated it. And he hated himself for having wanted to watch it.

After that, he didn't watch TV for a week. He wrote a letter to the TV station about the show. He wrote about it in his journal; he talked about it with his parents and with his friend Trevor. He even brought it up in class. Everyone agreed it was pretty terrible, but no one seemed to understand just how deeply Sloane felt about it. He couldn't shake it off. It made him ache in a place inside him he hadn't known was there. He wished he had never found that place.

———

Sometimes when things go bad, they get deeply rotten before they get better. That's what happened to Sloane. The new place inside him that ached so much for dead chipmunks and lion cubs got a real workout.

In his class, there was this girl, Cynthia, who had something wrong with her. Everyone liked her well enough but nobody really got to know her. She couldn't keep up with the class but the teacher didn't seem to worry too much about it. Cynthia was going to be having some operation; that was all any of the kids knew.

One Thursday Sloane's mother was going to be in town on an errand and so Sloane didn't take the school bus home that afternoon. He hung out at the park instead. He met a guy on the basketball court and they got talking and playing some one-on-one. The guy's name was Billy. It turned out that Billy was Cynthia's brother. When Sloane found out, he stopped right in the middle of dribbling towards the net. It was like the lion on TV all over again. He didn't want to ask but he couldn't stop himself.

"What's wrong with her?" he said. Billy told him. The operation was on her brain. It was pretty major. So Cynthia's family was trying to keep everything as ordinary as possible. That's why Cynthia was staying with her own age of kids in school even though she couldn't really keep up.

Billy bounced the ball a few times, watching the way the ball and its shadow met each time the ball hit the ground.

"Like last night," he said, "Mom made spaghetti and meatballs and when she gave Cyn her plate, Cyn said, 'Umm, this looks delicious. What is it?'"

Sloane wasn't sure he had heard right, wasn't sure he understood. "She never saw spaghetti and meatballs before?"

"Sure," said Billy. He bounced the ball a few times, never looking up. "We have it all the time."

Going home that night, Todd was whining a lot and Sloane was supposed to keep him entertained. Mother had a headache. Todd got more and more crotchety and Sloane grew angrier and angrier. He was thinking about Cynthia. How could such a thing happen? he kept thinking.

At home he got into a big argument with Lawren over whose turn it was to clean their room.

Rachel, his older sister, was making dinner that night. She made pumpkin lasagna. Everybody found other things to talk about. And then, suddenly, Sloane said, "It just isn't fair!"

Lawren thought he was talking about their room. Rachel thought he was talking about her pumpkin lasagna.

"Just 'cause the edges are a bit burnt," she said, and stamped out of the dining room.

Little Todd laughed. He liked the burnt edges.

Father excused himself and went to talk to Rachel.

"I meant something that happened in town," said Sloane.

"What?" said Lawren. "Did you see some more dead stuff?"

"Yeah, your brain," said Sloane.

"Boys!" said Mother.

But it was too late. Sloane couldn't hold back. He didn't want to talk about what Billy had told him. What good would talking do? He wished he had never heard of Cynthia. He wanted it all to go away.

He was sent to his room. Lawren slept somewhere else that night.

———

The next morning, when Sloane came down for breakfast, the family was excited. Father had seen an elk at the bottom of the garden while everyone was still asleep.

Although they lived in the country, on the edge of a forest, they had never heard of an elk being seen in the area. Sloane joined his brothers and sister looking out the window. But the elk was long gone.

"I was letting the cat in and the elk spooked when he heard the door open, took off into the brush," Father said. The family kidded him about it over breakfast, but they all knew he didn't make up stories.

"It was huge," he said. "Ten points on its rack."

"What?" Todd asked. Sloane explained to him that the elk had ten points on its antlers. It must have been a big one.

Little Todd wanted to see the elk. He asked Sloane to walk down to the bottom of the garden with him to look for it. Sloane was still depressed about Cynthia and the fight with Lawren. He hadn't slept well and he was grouchy, but he went anyway.

They went down and Sloane looked out at the forest, but he saw nothing more lively than the wind turning the leaves bellyside-up and a few noisy bluejays playing tag.

"I found his house!" Todd cried.

Sloane went to look. Todd was crouching beside a groundhog hole in the dirt bank where the lawn slipped off into bramble and prickly ash woodland.

"Whose house?" Sloane asked.

"The elk's," said Todd.

Sloane laughed. "An elk's huge," he said.

Todd poked at the hole with a stick. "Well, some of the dirt fell in so it doesn't look so big anymore."

Sloane laughed again. "No, I mean *huge* like a horse." He could see Todd staring at the hole and wondering how something as big as a horse could get into a hole so small.

"Come on," said Sloane, and he led his little brother back to the house. In an encyclopedia he showed him a picture of an elk.

Todd beamed and grabbed the book from his brother's hands. He tore out of the house and down to the groundhog hole. When Sloane arrived, Todd was comparing the size of the picture to the hole. He looked up triumphantly.

"See! It would so fit!"

Sloane shook his head. "You goof." He grabbed the encyclopedia. "Don't be so stupid!" he said, more angrily than he meant to. Then he headed back to the house to get his stuff for school.

He spent the day being sore and trying not to look at Cynthia or think about spaghetti. He got in trouble twice for not paying attention, once more for not having done his homework. He got a detention and had to take the late bus home from school.

As the bus neared his house, Sloane saw some of his neighbours walking along the sideroad. They had megaphones. He saw two police cars pulled over to the shoulder. There was another one in his driveway.

He rushed up to the house. That's when he found that Todd was missing.

"He was talking all morning about finding the elk's house," said Mother. Sloane went cold all over. There were search parties everywhere. Sloane could hear them down the old logging path, in the woods. "He's never wandered away before," said Mother. "He knows better than that!"

Sloane joined the search. The coldness that gripped him was like a black belt around his chest. As he tramped through the woods behind the house, moving deeper into the forest, the strap seemed to get tighter and tighter.

He didn't usually spend much time in the woods; he hardly ever had. City cousins who visited seemed to think he was lucky to live on the edge of a forest. They always wanted to play out there, to explore. They wanted to look for arrowheads and build forts. That was about the only time Sloane went into the woods anymore. He cursed it now for its rotten wildness, its thousand sharp edges, the pointlessness of it all.

And then suddenly he came to a place in the woods that he seemed to know. Maybe it was on one of those visits from city cousins that he had explored this particular part. He couldn't recall the time. Maybe, he thought later, he had known he was heading this way from the moment he left the house. The cries of the other searchers had fallen far behind, barely distinguishable now from the twittering and screeching of the birds.

An opening. There were several paths leading to it or from it depending on how you looked at things; where you had come from or where you were going.

Sloane stopped. It was as if he was in a dream. He felt he knew which path to take. He didn't know why, but the certainty of his decision seemed to loosen the belt around his chest a notch or two.

The path he chose led him through the dappled late afternoon into the shadow-making sunshine at the edge of a small meadow. Memory worked in him now. *He had been here!* When or how, he couldn't recall. The familiarity of the meadow was not a knowing thing so much as a feeling thing. As he walked, however, he was quite sure that he had been here alone.

Memory, loosed in him like this, seemed to unbuckle the fear and pain a few more notches. He stopped, looked around.

"This way," he told himself. "There will be an old fence. An abandoned road. A swamp. A junkyard."

He almost forgot Todd. It was as if he wasn't looking for him anymore. Almost.

Finally, Sloane saw what he had been looking for, though he could never have given it a name. In the junkyard, resting on no wheels, rusted and overgrown with thistles and harsh grasses, stood an old blue-grey panel truck. On the side of it in faded letters were the words: "The HOPE Bakery."

The words "The" and "Bakery" were in a swirly kind of script, but the word "HOPE" was printed in tall letters. There had once been a little hand-painted picture under this sign: some buns and loaves and a pie, maybe. It was hard to tell now. The paint was all peeled and crumbly.

Sloane looked at the panel truck, letting the shape of it drift into a waiting puzzle hole in his memory. And as he looked, the back door of the truck opened with a loud squeaking and out stepped Todd. Todd seemed almost to have been expecting him.

"You should see this, Sloaney," he called out, waving his hand. "I think this is where that elk lives."

Sloane made himself walk very slowly to his brother, as if to run might shatter the terrifying beauty of the moment. When he got there, he resisted hugging Todd, who was too busy anyway picking up rusted bits of engine parts, a stained hat, scraps of paper. If he hugged him, he was afraid he would burst into tears himself.

"There's plenty of room here," said the five-year-old. Sloane looked around, nodded.

Yes, he thought. Plenty of room.

TASHKENT

ONE day, for no particular reason, Fletcher pasted the names of a lot of exotic places on his chest and stomach. His mother and father were chatting in the kitchen when he went to show them.

"Oh, no," said his mother. "Fletcher's got the dreaded little-bits-of-paper-with-writing-on-it disease."

"There's been quite an outbreak of it," said his father, leaning close to inspect Fletcher's remarkably decorated torso. "Zagreb?"

"They're all places I'd like to go some day," said Fletcher, looking down at his chest. "When I'm older."

His mother joined in the examination. "Ibadan. Where's that?"

"It's the second largest city in Nigeria," said Fletcher, pressing down on that piece of paper. It was peeling already. He didn't want the names to fall off just yet, though they felt funny on his skin now that the glue had dried.

Dad went to refill his coffee cup. "How long is this malady going to last?"

Mom, always more matter-of-fact, said, "What about gym?"

"Gym's not until Thursday," said Fletcher. "They should have all fallen off by then."

Even as he spoke, Ibadan fluttered to the floor. They all watched. Mom picked it up but wasn't sure what you did when the second biggest city in Nigeria fell on your kitchen floor. She handed it to Fletcher, who crumpled it up and put it in his pants pocket.

"The last place left is the first place I'm going to travel to when I'm old enough," said Fletcher.

Dad stopped pouring his coffee for a moment. "So it's sort of a contest?" he said.

Mom frowned. "Does this contest stretch all the way down into your shorts?"

"Nope," said Fletcher. He turned and carefully headed out of the kitchen, walking like a robot so as not to disturb the possibilities stuck all over him. "That wouldn't be fair."

"Not fair?"

Fletcher turned at the door, twisting slowly from the waist. "I mean, if I put—let's say—Bilbao on my heel, it would come off the first time I pulled on my sock, right?" His mother and father nodded. "And if I put Uppsala on my bum —"

"We get the idea," said Mom.

"Yes," said Dad. "Now it all makes perfect sense."

Fletcher smiled. He had a winning smile.

When he was nine, Fletcher almost died. He got sick, and it wasn't the little-bits-of-paper-with-writing-on-it disease. Nobody was able to figure out what it was. He just got weaker and weaker.

The medical people did x-rays and found nothing. They did "blood-work," as they called it, and found nothing. They did ultrasound; they squilched goop all over his abdomen, and a technician pushed something like a computer mouse through the goop. Somehow or other Fletcher's insides appeared on a TV monitor. The technician watched the monitor closely. So did Fletcher.

"That ugly thing must be it," he said at one point.

"That's your kidney," the technician said. "It looks fine to me."

Fletcher asked the technician if he could tune in the Cosby Show. The technician laughed. The ultrasound found nothing.

Fletcher had to be very brave because, as far as he knew, he was dying. He seemed to have no immunities to anything. They tested for AIDS, but it wasn't AIDS. They wanted to open him up and see what was going on, but by then Fletcher had become too weak, and the doctors were afraid that the operation would kill him. That's when Fletcher learned the expression "between a rock and a hard place."

As the months of his mysterious illness dragged on and he sank lower and lower, he talked to his mother a lot about death. Death became a place. Like Death Valley in California. Or Death Valley Junction, the last place before Death Valley. It didn't hurt so much to think about death if it was somewhere to visit, even if it was quite far away from anywhere else. That's when Fletcher started looking at atlases and travel books a lot and thinking about exotic places that weren't quite so hard to take.

———

"Why are you clutching your gut?" said Shlomo when they were walking to school the next day. Shlomo was Fletcher's best friend. He looked worried.

Fletcher explained about the exotic places stuck all over his body. Shlomo looked relieved.

"I thought I saw a little piece of paper drop off you a while back."

"Did you happen to notice what it said?" Fletcher asked. Even though he had slept on his back with only his sheet over him, he had lost both Singapore and Tunapuna during the night.

Shlomo hadn't noticed what city it was. Fletcher hoped it wasn't somewhere warm. The warm places were dropping like flies. Not that he really cared which city won. He'd get to them all anyway. It was just a matter of where to start.

Fletcher gave Shlomo a winning smile. Shlomo frowned.

"I've been meaning to talk to you about this stupid smiling thing," he said.

———

After a year of his mysterious illness, they put Fletcher in a hospital for a few weeks. But he seemed to get worse, so they sent him home again.

They tried some medicines — some real ones and some pretend ones, just in case he was faking it. None of them made the slightest difference.

Then, after two years, when he could do little more than lie in bed, think of faraway places and imagine packing his bags, suddenly Fletcher started to get better. It took most of a year. His appetite came back. His colour came back. The only thing he didn't get back was the three years his mysterious illness had stolen from him.

By the time Fletcher returned to school, he was twelve, although he looked nine. But he was smart and he'd studied at home while he was sick, so they put him in the sixth grade.

But before he went back to school, the medical people decided that, since he was fine now, it might be good to do that exploratory operation they hadn't been able to do earlier when he had been too weak. So they opened him up.

And what they found was a battlefield.

That's how the head-surgeon described it. The inside of Fletcher's abdomen was like a scarred battlefield. Fletcher thought of his guts now as a place covered with empty helmets and wrecked swords and shields, all the size of Playmobil stuff but not in primary colours. Rusty. Stained. Whatever had been in him was gone, driven away by the soldiers of Fletcher's own inner power. That's how the head-surgeon put it.

So it wasn't that Fletcher had no immunities. He had *amazing* immunities! His immunities had taken on something pretty terrible and licked it on the battlefield of his abdominal cavity.

As he was convalescing from the operation, Fletcher enjoyed thinking about his amazing immunities. It was nice to have a talent. In between worrying about going to a new school with kids he hadn't seen much of in three years and who looked three years older than him, he liked thinking about those Soldiers of His Own Inner Power.

———

Fletcher didn't hate school, but it was a little difficult to cope with after lying around dying for three years. But he was alive and that was so much better than the alternative. So he smiled a lot at school. He smiled at his desk, at his homework assignment, at his classmates. He even smiled at the soup in the cafeteria—even when it was green.

Some people thought he was cuckoo. Some people thought he really was nine and that he was a genius.

One person wanted to smash his face in with a brick.

That's what Ted Sawchuk said. "You wanna get your face smashed in with a brick?" He said it, Shlomo explained later, because Fletcher had smiled at Vivian Weir, who Ted considered to be his girl.

"You've got to watch that, Fletch," Shlomo said. Fletcher couldn't quite figure out what it was he was supposed to watch. He'd missed some of this stuff while he was dying.

The incident with Ted had been two weeks ago. Today as they walked to school with Fletcher feeling all those prickly places under his shirt, Shlomo tried to explain to him again about how much people like Ted hated people with winning smiles.

That wasn't Fletcher's only problem this morning. He realized that maybe the exotic place names all over his body might better have been a weekend thing to do. They itched, but if he scratched, it would be an unfair advantage to a place that didn't itch. He looked uncomfortable. The teacher noticed and asked him if he was all right. The teacher looked frightened and annoyed at the same time, like someone who didn't want a kid dying in his classroom.

Fletcher lost Anchorage and Reykjavik at recess, which made up for losing the hot places in bed. Shlomo hurriedly picked up any bits of paper near his friend in case anybody noticed.

"I feel a bit like a leper," said Fletcher.

"Like a leopard?" Shlomo asked.

"No," said Fletcher. "A leper. When bits of your skin fall off. Your nose, an ear."

Shlomo shivered. "Here!" he said and shoved the bit of paper with Reykjavik written on it into Fletcher's pocket.

Just then Ted passed by and glared at Fletcher. Fletcher smiled back.

Ted snarled but kept moving,

"I told you not to do that," said Shlomo.

"I can't help it," said Fletcher.

Vivian Weir was in music class with Fletcher. Ted wasn't. Fletcher tried not to smile at her. This only made things worse, because he looked like he was holding in a big joke. Vivian had never seemed to mind him smiling in her direction, but now she wasn't sure if he was laughing at her. She hid her face behind her saxophone.

———

It wasn't until the next day after school that Ted caught up with Fletcher in the hall. He jostled him heavily into the wall. The lockers groaned. As Fletcher got up, a piece of paper slipped out of his shirt and helicoptered to the floor like a maple key. Fletcher reached for it, but Ted put his fat, black boot on the slip of paper.

"Some of your brains fell out," he said as he bent to pick up the paper from under his shoe. It was stuck to a piece of chewing gum and he couldn't read it. The chewing gum made him mad, as if Fletcher was responsible for where he walked.

"He wouldn't have been able to read it anyway," said Shlomo later.

———

"How goes the battle?" said Fletcher's father. He was standing at Fletcher's bedroom door. Fletcher was stripped to the waist examining himself in the mirror over his dresser. Shlomo was lying on the bed reading Calvin and Hobbes.

"Only five places left," said Shlomo proudly, as if Fletcher was a show horse and he was its trainer.

"So I see," said Fletcher's father. But Fletcher could see in the mirror that his father's eyes were staring at the scar left from the exploratory surgery. Fletcher rubbed it gently with his finger, careful not to touch the exotic place that was closest to it.

"Does it still itch?" his father asked, kneeling on the floor to look more closely.

"Only sometimes," said Fletcher.

Shlomo crawled over to take a closer look himself. "Tashkent," he said. "Where's that?"

"In the republic of Uzbek," said Fletcher. "In the foothills of the Tien Shan Mountains."

"Get out!" said Shlomo, grinning. "Why couldn't you just memorize batting averages?"

"And if Tashkent wins," said Fletcher's father, "you'll actually go there?"

Fletcher smiled at the three faces in the mirror. "Don't worry," he said. "I'll write."

Only the city of Sofia fell that night, so Fletcher entered the school yard Thursday morning with four contenders left. Four corners of the world. Four places that were as yet only names and a few odd facts to him but would one day be strong smells and handsome faces and clanging noises that he had never heard before.

Someone pushed by him when the bell rang and dislodged Kowloon. And in setting up the screen for a movie about teeth, he jabbed himself and lost Rangoon.

Shlomo could hardly contain himself over lunch. "Let me see. Are they still there?"

And Fletcher would stare down the inside of his sweater at the two finalists and say, "Yes, they're still there."

Shlomo was acting like a drake honking around the nest where two eggs were about to hatch.

Fletcher was pretty excited himself. Too excited to remember *not* to smile at Vivian Weir when she passed by his table with her lunch tray. She smiled back. She had a pretty winning smile herself.

Then he and Shlomo went out to the school yard, and Ted was on them like a ton of bricks.

"Some guys never learn," he said, pushing Fletcher and heaving him backwards into the dirt so hard that Fletcher's hand smashed against a rock and got badly scraped. He ended up in that hard place where the playground ends and the fence begins.

"He's hurt," said one of the people who gathered around. A girl dropped Fletcher a Kleenex.

Shlomo didn't stop to think about it. He just started punching Ted, forgetting all about how big Ted was. "The guy almost died," he said. "Why don't you pick on someone who didn't almost die."

Ted pushed Shlomo off. "Because," he said, "if people almost die they should be more careful who they smile at when they start living again."

Fletcher dabbed at his hand. The Kleenex was soaked. He looked at Vivian through the crowd. He tried to tell her in that complicated language of facial muscles going every which way at the same time that he liked to smile, that he liked to smile at her, but that it didn't mean anything. And if it did, what of it, because it was only a way of being nervous and happy to be alive all jumbled up into a thing the face did without having to say anything.

Fletcher tried to tell Vivian with his face that he was going to travel to faraway places where smiling winningly might be the only form of communication left, and that he was practising on people with whom more advanced forms of communication like talking or joking around were out of the question, being that he looked like a nine-year-old among a forest of twelve-year-olds.

He tried to say something like that. Vivian nodded. She looked pretty confused, but she seemed to understand.

Meanwhile, the crowd around Ted and Fletcher was talking. They weren't generally pleased with Ted. "Leave the guy alone," somebody said. "He's just a little cuckoo."

"Cuckoo? Fletcher's a genius!" said someone else.

And then Shlomo, who had recovered from being pushed and was just about to attack Ted again, turned to see how his friend was doing and saw a tiny strip of paper on the ground.

"All right!" he said, diving for it. On his knees he cleaned it off, smoothed it out. The crowd crowded nearer. People said things like "What is it?" "Did some more of his brain fall out?" and things like that.

Shlomo read, "Dar-something . . . Dar es-something . . ."

"Dar es Salaam," said Fletcher. "Founded by the sultan of Zanzibar in 1866."

Then, with everyone looking really confused and kind of left out and Shlomo whooping with laughter, Fletcher pulled up his sweater to reveal the last place in the world left sticking to him: the first place in the world he would journey to when he was older. It was right next to his scar.

Of course. He was always so careful about that part of his body. There was a battlefield under there.

"What is this garbage?" said Ted. Reaching down, he ripped the last piece of paper off Fletcher's body. "Tashkent," he read. "Who's that, Clark's brother?"

Some people laughed. The crowd kind of eased up.

"It's in Uzbek," said Shlomo. "In the shadow of the Tien Shan Mountains."

"Well, in the foothills, anyway," said Fletcher, laughing. The crowd laughed some more, too. Fletcher noticed Vivian laughing prettily. Ted was the only angry person around.

"So what's it doing sticking to you?" he said. "You get too close?" Some of Ted's friends har-har-harred which seemed to loosen a few of the angry knots in his face.

"Not yet," said Fletcher. "Here. Give me a hand." He said it directly to Ted, but Ted was holding Tashkent, so other hands helped Fletcher up from the ground. Somebody dusted him off.

Ted looked around. One of his friends shrugged. Ted shook his head, shrugged himself, and shoved the paper with Tashkent written on it at Fletcher. When Fletcher took it, Ted noticed his bleeding hand.

"You gonna die on us again?" he asked.

"Nope," said Fletcher. "I'm just going to travel far, far away."

STRANGERS
ON THE SHORE

ACKER Bilk. Whoever named a baby Acker Bilk?

Harry was going through his father's old records. He looked at the picture on the cover of the man playing the clarinet. He tried to imagine the man without a beard, as a kid named Acker.

"Hey, Acker. How's it goin'?"

"Okay, Harry. You?"

Then Harry wondered if maybe Acker Bilk came from a place where lots of kids were called Acker. Maybe there had been two or three of them in his class, like all the Justins in Harry's class. There weren't any other Harrys. Harry was Harry's dad's name and his father's before that. Maybe Acker's father had been an Acker, too.

Harry imagined phoning the Bilk residence.

"Hi. Is Acker there?"

"Well, that depends. You want Acker Junior or Acker Senior? Old man Acker's dead, of course, so it couldn't be him you're after."

Harry slipped the record — his father called them LPs—out of its sleeve. It was old but in mint condition. When his father had first said that one of his records was in mint condition, Harry had thought maybe it would smell like toothpaste. But it just meant that Dad was careful with records. He cleaned them with a special cloth; cleaned the needle with a special fluid applied with a special little brush. It was like something holy.

On his knees Harry placed the holy LP on the holy turntable. There was only a little bit of a hiss — what Dad called surface noise.

"Strangers on the Shore." There were no words, just old Acker pumping on the clarinet and 400,000 violins sawing away in the background. It was really mushy. Harry lay on the rug with his hands cradling his head and listened to the syrupy sweet music under the holy surface noise.

There was a girl about Harry's age who lived in the apartment next door to his father's. They had met once at the mailroom in the lobby. Her name was Flower.

Harry thought about knocking on her door. He thought about inviting Flower over to listen to Acker Bilk. He could imagine her laughing at that. She was the only Flower in her class. She had a brother named Night. He was the only Night in his class. And Harry was the only Harry.

They could form a club, he thought, and invite Acker to be the honorary president. Harry imagined Flower listening to "Strangers on the Shore," sitting on the rug leaning against the couch. "Not too much surface noise," he might say to her. She might be impressed. They would need something to talk about. Harry wasn't good at talking to people.

———◆———

Earlier that day, one hundred and twenty-three kilometres away from Harry's dad's apartment in the city, Cluny Smith waited for the school bus in the miniature covered bus shelter her father had made for her at the end of the driveway.

Cluny lived in the woods, and their driveway was as long as most people's streets. Her father had made the shelter out of rounded slabs of cedar logs. It was only big enough for a seat and Cluny. Sometimes she thought about decorating it with wallpaper and posters. She thought about putting up shelves with a book or two, a picture of her dog, a vase. She imagined having her own little TV there, a mini-fridge. She thought the same thought every school morning while she sat waiting for the bus but never remembered about it when she got home in the afternoon.

But this morning Cluny's mind was on other things. Her mind was on the first issue of her very own magazine. It was called *Cluny: The Magazine for People with Weird Names*. The lead article started like this:

Hi! I know you're out there. And now, here's a magazine just for you!

There followed a recipe for Scheherezade Casserole which she had got from the *Moosewood Cook Book*; a little bit of a story about Scheherezade and the One Thousand and One Tales of the Arabian Nights; and then a contest: how many words can you make out of the name Scheherezade? Her dad had suggested that a contest was a good idea for the first issue of a magazine because it invited people to write in, get involved. Her dad ought to know. He produced his own magazine right out of the house. It was an ecology magazine called *Turnip*. Actually, he called *Turnip* a zeen, a short form for magazine. A zeen didn't have advertising in it and it didn't appear on newsstands, but every month her dad wrote and printed up about one thousand copies and mailed them out himself all over the place.

People heard about *Turnip* by word of mouth. They sent in donations if they felt like it. Mostly they sent in articles which Dad put in the next issue. Cluny's dad didn't make any money producing *Turnip* but, as Cluny's mother put it, "In the Smith household, John raises the consciences and I raise the cash." Her mom worked at an ordinary job that she liked. Mom also liked the fact that when John was finished raising consciences for the day, he cleaned house and raised a little supper.

John had let Cluny print her own zeen on the laser printer. It looked pretty professional. She had printed ten copies. She had them with her in a shopping bag. She was going to give two each to her friends: Percy, Bryony and Darwin. The idea was that they would hand out a magazine each to someone else with a weird name.

Cluny took a copy out of the shopping bag and looked it over for the umpteenth time. After the

Scheherezade stuff there was a poem, "archy and mehitabel," written by Don Marquis. The poem was supposed to have been written by archy, a very literary cockroach, in Marquis' office at the newspaper where he worked. archy was obliged to write without capital letters because he couldn't operate the shift key on the typewriter. mehitabel was archy's friend, a cat. It was because of mehitabel that Cluny had included the poem in her first issue. mehitabel was a very weird name.

Because the first issue of the magazine was coming out on November 19th, there was also a birthday greeting to Saint Mechtilde of Hackeborn. Mechtilde had been born in 1241, and November 19th was her saint day, if it wasn't exactly her birthday. Nobody really knew her birthday. Cluny had found out about her in a dictionary of saints. She'd written a little story about Saint Mechtilde and what great things she had done. And after it, Cluny had added in italics: *So you see, even if you have a weird name like Mechtilde, you can still accomplish big things!*

Cluny stood up as she heard the bus coming. She was nervous. She really hoped *Cluny* would go over well.

The bus stopped and she climbed on board.

"How'd it come out?" asked the bus driver.

"Okay," said Cluny. "Here's your copies, Percy." She handed the bus driver the very first two copies of the very first issue of her very own zeen.

"Hey, Clueless!" yelled someone from the back of the bus. "Got one for me?"

Percy rolled his eyes and started looking at the magazine. "Very nice," he said.

"Don't start reading it now," said Cluny. Old Percy's driving was bad enough without a new distraction!

———◆———

Every second Friday, Harry took a train from his mother's city to his father's. He got to miss school all of Friday and Monday morning, too. There had been a lot of wrangling about this arrangement, because Harry was only twelve, for God's sake. But he was a reliable kind of kid and a good student, and there were all sorts of safety precautions to make sure he didn't get lost and end up in Bolivia, for God's sake, and it had all worked out. He had a thousand phone numbers on him and emergency money, just in case, but he had never had to use either.

Harry liked to think about having an emergency. He liked the idea of having to use the emergency money. The train trip lasted just over an hour. Mostly it took him through rocky land and muskeg and cedar forests with little pastures cut out of them for a few sheep or cows. You couldn't see many towns from the train. It would be hard to spend emergency money out there.

Harry took a cab from the train station to his dad's apartment. His dad usually got off work at about two o'clock on Fridays, which gave them extra time together. Usually Harry didn't have to wait too long before his dad arrived home, but sometimes he was late.

By the time Harry discovered "Strangers on the Shore," it was already 4:30. With no word from his father, Harry began to wonder if there was some problem. He began to wonder if he might finally get a chance to break into his emergency funds. He imagined having to buy his own supper and a few videos, maybe.

He stood at the window of his dad's apartment and looked down at the street seventeen floors below. He tried to make out his dad amid the ants down there. They were all going somewhere in a big Friday-afternoon hurry.

He stopped listening to Acker Bilk. He put on Billy Vaughan and his Orchestra. Instead of 400,000 violins, this LP featured 400,000 saxophones, all playing the same melody. Very slowly. It was just as mushy and boring as "Strangers on the Shore."

Harry thought of phoning his dad's office, but the secretary always called him Junior and asked him how he was. She expected a real answer. She wanted to have a conversation with him. So Harry just listened to the LP, instead. LP stood for Long Playing. The way Billy Vaughan played it seemed very long. It grew dark.

At 5:38 his dad phoned. He was still in an unexpected meeting that was really important. He said he was sorry. He said he would bring home a pizza. He said to look through the papers and see what was playing and pick a movie. Harry picked a movie, but when his father came home at seven he brought not only a pizza but a friend from the office. She was a lot of fun. They all made a crazy salad together, but they never did get to the movie.

———

Cluny Smith's father's name was John. Her mother's name was Anne. Cluny was named after a museum in Paris where her parents had met. Her mom and dad kidded her that if they had had other children they would have named them after museums, too, so Cluny wouldn't feel so weird. Cluny tried to imagine having a brother named Ashmolean, or Smithsonian. Smithsonian Smith! It might make a funny piece for the second issue of *Cluny*.

By Friday afternoon the zeen was well and truly launched. Percy was going to send a copy to his sister, Irene. Irene wasn't that uncommon a name in the old days, but you didn't see too much of it about anymore, he told Cluny. He made it sound like smallpox or some old-fashioned disease. There was another reason he was sending Irene the magazine. "She lives in Punky Doodle Corner." Cluny gave him the big thumbs up.

Bryony was sending her extra copy to her friend Hezekiah who lived in California. Hez was named after an ancient king of Judah, and Bryony had the idea that they could include weird biblical names in the next issue of the zeen: Nahor and Uz and Pildash, things like that. She had looked up the names in the library. Maybe they could make it a regular feature.

Darwin didn't know anybody with a weird name other than Bry and Cluny, but he was going to draw a picture of the baseball player Rance Mulliniks for the second issue. It was a good start.

Or it should have been.

But Kelly O'Connor, who had tried to snatch a copy of the magazine as soon as Cluny had got on the bus that morning, finally managed to get hold of one in the bus line-up after school. She grabbed it right out of the bag in Cluny's arms, and when she did she ripped the bag, and two copies of the magazine fell on the ground and got covered with muck. Then Kelly sat at the back of the bus all the way home reading it out loud to her friends. Cluny covered her ears. It all sounded stupid coming from the likes of Kelly and Susan and Crystal and Tracy. "Clowny Magazine," they called it; the magazine for people who have nothing better to do.

What did they know about it.

———

It was not a good weekend for Harry. Sometimes that happened. He had gotten pretty good at figuring out when a weekend with Dad wasn't going to be a good one. The Friday meeting that had kept his father at the office had to be reconvened on Saturday afternoon, which meant the track and field meet at the coliseum was out. Harry's father kept thinking of people Harry could go to it with. Harry said he would be all right at the apartment. He didn't really feel like going anyway. His father said, "Well, if that's the way you're going to be about it."

Harry ended up listening to LPs. Lester Lanin. Nat King Cole. Dizzy Gillespie.

He was making himself a sandwich when he heard a noise down the hall. He ran to the door in time to see Flower stepping into her apartment.

"Hi," he called.

"Hi, Harry," she called back and waved. Then a guy who was not Night and who Harry had not seen before poked his head out her door and said, "Hi, Harry," and a couple of other kids did the same and called him Harry as if they knew him. Then they all went into Flower's place and closed the door. Harry sat in a chair with a comic, practising looking as if he was having a fine time and hoping Flower might knock on his door and invite him to the party if he had nothing better to do.

His dad got home tired at six. They watched a hockey game on the tube. The Canucks lost.

Sunday, Harry's dad was still tired. They went for a walk down the canal that ran through the city. It was cold and wet. They had lunch out at a restaurant Harry's dad liked. Harry's burger had sprouts on it. It was that kind of a weekend.

That night while they cleaned up after supper, Harry asked if the friend from the office would be around again. His dad said he wasn't sure. Harry said, "Well, she sure knows how to make a crazy salad." But his dad didn't laugh.

Harry said he would put on some music to wash dishes by. He chose "Strangers on the Shore." He thought it would make his dad a little happier. He wiped the record first with the special cloth and cleaned the needle with the special brush that he had dipped in the special liquid. But his hand slipped as he lowered the needle arm and it jumped right out of his hand hard onto the LP.

"For God's sake, Harry!" said his father. "Please be careful."

They washed in silence to the sound of 400,000 violins and one syrupy clarinet. They both tried hard not to hear the new bit of surface noise that had not been there before.

———

One hundred and twenty-three kilometres away, Cluny's weekend was lousy, too. Someone delivered an anonymous letter to her door early on Saturday.

Dear Loony,
I was so glad to see a magazine for people like us. My friend Frogetta wants to subscribe. She has nothing to do most of the time cos she's a real stick-in-the-mud. Also my friend Frankfurter is interested in your magazine. He's a real wiener. I hope you will have a joke section. Here's one. Q: How many people with weird names does it take to screw in a lightbulb? A: None. They'd rather be in the dark. Ha. Ha. Ha. Anyway, have to run cos my boyfriend Pizzaface is at the door. So long for now,

Yours most sincerely,

Lulu McDinkus-Puss

Ha. Ha. Ha.

Dad told Cluny that you had to expect cranks. He showed her a file folder full of stupid letters people had sent to *Turnip*. You get used to it, he said. Cluny wasn't so sure. He didn't have to get on a school bus five days a week.

By Monday morning, Cluny couldn't understand why she had ever decided to do such a dumb thing. By Monday morning she was wondering whether she was going to risk taking the bus or work up a quick case of flu. Mom suggested that a quick case of flu wasn't going to get rid of Kelly and Susan and Crystal and Tracy.

"Besides, having an original name builds character," she said.

"How about a deathly case of flu?" Cluny asked.

Mom gave her one of her looks. Her looks were like her coffee, black with no sugar. Cluny gathered her stuff together.

———

Harry's dad drove him to the train station Monday morning, and when he hugged him goodbye he promised to make up for the lousy weekend next time. The train pulled out of the station. It was raining and cold. Harry leaned his forehead against the window. It was 8:15.

———

Cluny waited for the school bus. She had her school books, lunch and one copy of *Cluny*, well hidden. She was only taking it because her teacher wanted to read it. Fame.

The bus came and even before it stopped, Cluny could hear that the noise was worse than ever. Percy opened the door for her. The noise was deafening. He pointed to his ears. He had cotton batting in them.

"Clue-less-Loo-ny! Clue-less-Loo-ny!"

Percy winced.

Cluny tried to remind herself that the chant was coming from a handful of witless goofballs, that most of the people on this bus were okay, that some of them were genuinely friendly and didn't care what her name was, that it would all die down and be forgotten and the witless goofballs would find someone else to pick on. She sat down, her face burning, trying very hard to remind herself of all this. But all she could think of was the copy of *Cluny* tucked between her notes. And the magazine, despite anything she tried to tell herself, shrank and shrank and shrank in her mind's eye until it was nothing but a bright, hot ember. An idea who's time had gone. No matter what her folks said about cranks or character, nothing—*nothing*—was worth this.

She stared at poor old Percy's bald head. His shoulders were hunched up around his ears. Even with the cotton batting the noise was too much for him.

"Clue-less-Loo-ny! Clue-less-Loo-ny!"

She refused to cover her own ears. And so it was that she heard that other sound, a sound bigger than the chanting, a sound as big as her thumping heart. A sound coming out of nowhere. She didn't have time to think of it as a train. She was still staring at Percy's head when it hit the bus.

"It's all right!" said the train conductor. "No one seems to be too badly hurt. *Personne n'a été blessé,*" he added, so that the passengers would be reassured in both official languages.

Harry stared from his window back down the track to the level crossing where the school bus stood, its front end almost entirely torn off and twisted. Kids were being herded out of the bus, one or two supported by others but no one carried out, so far. The driver was sitting on the ground. Train men and women were squatting and standing around him. He seemed to be talking. *Personne n'a été blessé.*

Passengers from the other side of the train crowded around Harry trying to catch a glimpse of the bus — the accident — three hundred metres down the track. It had taken the train that long to stop.

"The bus driver stopped and then went ahead right into the path of the train," one passenger said. He had heard it from someone who had heard it from the conductor who had heard it from the engineer.

"Lucky those school buses don't go very fast," said someone else.

"But these trains sure do," said someone else again. "A real close call!"

Harry got up from his seat and squirmed his way through the crowd.

"Probably going to be sick," he heard someone say quietly, as he made his way to the end of the car. "Such a shock. Poor kid."

But Harry didn't feel sick. What he saw through the window made him feel alive all over. What he saw through the window was an emergency.

He found his knapsack on the shelves at the car's end and, taking one last look at his fellow passengers, he heaved it over his shoulder, pushed open the door between the cars and made his way down the unguarded steps to the gravel bed of the track.

The air smelled strongly of engine, pulsating heat, oil and escaping steam. Harry shivered and hurried down the siding towards the level crossing. He didn't look back in case someone called him and made him return to his seat.

"There's nothing on this ticket about getting off and having adventures," he imagined the conductor saying. He imagined him saying it in both official languages. But by then he was at the scene of the accident, just another school kid in the rain. He didn't look hurt. No one paid any attention to him.

Up close he could see that some of the kids had cuts and bruises. One kid was crying hard and holding his arm in a funny way. A train man was unrolling bandage from a first-aid kit. Another kid was lying on the ground; he had fainted. Down the dirt road Harry saw flashing lights and then heard the siren of an ambulance coming towards them.

It was going to be all right. Big kids were helping little kids. Two guys were playing catch with an apple. A girl in the thick wiry grass by the side of the dirt road was crying hysterically. Another girl was holding her, consoling her.

"It's okay, Kelly," said the girl. "Calm down."

"Can I help?" Harry asked. The hysterical girl, Kelly, hid her head in the other girl's shoulder and held onto her tightly. Harry didn't know what to do. He patted Kelly on the shoulder.

"You'll be okay," he said in a reassuring way. Kelly stopped crying immediately and stole a glance at this stranger. She looked horrible. She had a bad scratch on her forehead and her eyes were all puffy from crying. The rain drizzled down her face. The other girl smiled a little at Harry and patted Kelly's head.

Then the ambulance arrived and one of the train men called for all the children with injuries to come. Kelly, with a final sob, left the girl who had held her. As she left she squeezed the girl's hand.

"She'll be okay," said Harry. It seemed a stupid thing to say. He looked at the girl to see if she thought it was a stupid thing to say. She didn't seem to have noticed.

"Who are you?" she asked.

Harry told her he had just gotten off the train. He told her where he had been and where he was going.

The girl laughed. "Don't you have a name?" she asked.

"Harry," he said, feeling stupider than ever.

"Cluny," said the girl, shaking his hand.

She wanted to get her books from the bus. Harry walked with her. But the police had arrived and no one could go on the bus. So Cluny started walking away down the road. Nobody seemed to notice except Harry.

"Where are you going?" he asked.

"Home," she said. "It's just a kilometre. Bye, Harry. Thanks for your help."

"It was nothing," said Harry, nodding. He waved to her. He turned to look at the accident. He looked at the train. It didn't seem like such a big adventure anymore. Nobody looked at him. He turned and watched Cluny walking away. He watched her for about one whole minute.

"Cluny," he called. She turned. He ran after her. "Maybe I could call my mother from your place," he said, a little out of breath. "She always says not to hesitate to call if there is any kind of emergency." He said it in his mother's voice, and Cluny laughed, as if she had heard a voice like that before. She had a great laugh.

"Okay, Harry," she said.

Harry fell in step beside her.

He began to feel very, very pleased with himself. There were woods on either side of the road. He realized that it was raining in the woods but not raining on him anymore, on the road, on them. Step by step the sound of the accident fell behind them, until all he could hear was the rain and the wind soughing in the cedars. It sounded like 400,000 violins.

"Cluny," he said. "That's a beautiful name."

TWEEDLEDUM
AND
TWEEDLEDEAD

"IT'S a commando raid on Wonderland," said Tobias.

Peach rolled her eyes. "This is your assignment?" she asked. "You're going to hand this in?"

Tobias looked at his notebook. Maybe he shouldn't have shown the story to Peach before it was finished. Something in him had said to keep it under his hat, but he had to show someone. Someone he trusted.

Now that someone had handed his story back without finishing the first page.

"It's this guy—"

"Sergeant Steele."

"Yeah. And he hates *Alice in Wonderland*. At the end you find out that his parents forced the book down his throat when he was a kid. He really wanted to play outside, but they made him read instead. So now he has found out by grilling this weasely counterspy that there is a Wonderland. It actually exists. It's Top Secret. So he gets these guys together—"

"The Desperate Throng," said Peach. "I like that. It's good." Peach said "throng" a few times, throwing it off her teeth with her tongue. "The-wrong, the-wrong, the-wrong."

"Right," said Tobias, "and they plan this raid."

Peach rolled her eyes again. That was part of the reason she liked Tobias. No one gave her more reason to roll her eyes, and it was her best trick.

"Just tell me this," she said. "Does Alice live?"

Toby's eyes gave him away. Peach panicked. "No! Don't say it!" She snatched the notebook out of his hands and, holding it up in front of his eyes, prepared to tear it in half.

"What are you doing?"

"Alice has to live!" said Peach. "Maybe this Steele guy doesn't realize it, but he's in love with her, or something, so he saves her life."

"And if he doesn't?" said Tobias, trying to say it the way Sergeant Steele would say it — spitting it out like a piece of gristle.

"Then you end up with two *short* stories, Toby," said Peach. There was menace in her voice.

Tobias smiled like Steele. "Since when could you rip a notebook in half?"

Since my uncle Mike showed me," said Peach, stepping out of reach. "It's all in the wrists. You just tear one page at a time—that's the trick of it. Mike can rip a phone book in half this way. It's going to become my new best trick."

Tobias took a step towards her and she started to tear. He stopped dead in his tracks.

"All I need is a bit of practice," said Peach. Tobias retreated, holding up his hands like a guy in a movie to show he had no weapons on him.

Peach shook her head. "You can't go around shooting people and bombing them," she said.

"It's just a story."

"It's more like a dumb video game. Alice is special, Toby."

"I know."

"No, you don't. She's not all syrupy like in the Disney movie. That's all you know. She's tough. She doesn't take anything from anybody. You'd like her if you knew her. I seriously don't think you want to trash her, okay?"

Toby knew a threat when he heard one. He gave in. And Peach handed him back the notebook.

"Read *Alice in Wonderland* sometime," she said. Tobias didn't promise anything.

The assignment topic was "What I did on my summer vacation." Amelia had petted a stingray in the Monterey Aquarium. Graham had caught a foul ball at a Blue Jays game. He had the ball to prove it.

Then it was time for Tobias to read about his summer vacation adventure. He read "Tweedledum and Tweedledead: An Eyewitness Report." In only two pages, Sergeant Steele and the Desperate Throng wiped out Wonderland without a hitch. It was brutal. They turned the caterpillar into caterpillar dust, stuffed the Mad Hatter into his own hat and left the rabbit who had started the whole thing twitching in a ditch. Steele kept the rabbit's gold watch. Tweedledum and Tweedledee tried to round up some help from beyond the looking-glass, but they got wasted by one of the commandos, Mad Clyde and his flame-thrower. Alice was spared. She was carried home in a basket by the Desperate Throng and put in a special zoo with Winnie-the-Pooh, Wilbur the pig and the Cat in the Hat.

Nervously, Tobias looked at Ms. Julia Peach to see if she approved of his revised ending. She gave him the thumbs up.

Ms. Knieppe, however, did not. She invited Tobias to the front, took the story from him and reread it to herself.

She said she was appalled.

She asked if anyone knew what appalled meant. The class nodded its head. They could tell what she meant from the look on her face. But Ms. Knieppe didn't stop there. With Tobias still standing at the front, she got the class to try to spell it.

Amelia got it right. Amelia got to look it up in the dictionary: *appall v.t. to fill with dismay or horror; terrify; shock.*

Which was exactly what the class had seen on Ms. Knieppe's face.

Ms. Knieppe scribbled a note and invited Tobias to take his story to Mrs. Armitage, the principal, to see what she thought of it. Tobias snuck a peek at Peach as he left the room. She was rolling her eyes to beat the band.

Tobias sat outside the principal's office in a little dead-end hallway off the main office. In the main office the fall sun streamed through the window. One of the secretaries, Mrs. Devlin, was chatting to a man in a uniform who had delivered some packages. She was having a coffee and telling him about the trouble she was having with her K-Car. It turned out that the man in the uniform had had the same kind of trouble.

The school nurse smiled at Tobias as she got some stuff from her mailbox. And Ms. Rowanook of the orange hair was typing something with a Sony Walkman on, bobbing her head to the music.

It gave Tobias a nice cheery feeling to see everybody having a good time. It gave him hope.

Mrs. Armitage, meanwhile, was on the phone. Tobias could just make her out through the pebbled glass of her door. He could hear bits and pieces of what she was saying. Mrs. Devlin had taken in "Tweedledum and Tweedledead" with the note from Ms. Knieppe, and right away Mrs. Armitage had got on the phone.

At first Tobias thought she was phoning his parents or the cops or something, but the phone call didn't seem to have anything to do with him. So he waited in the dead-end hall, just out of the sunshine, until finally Mrs. Armitage hung up.

His waiting changed then. His ears filled up with the silence of her reading his story. He was Sergeant Steele holding his breath, hiding in a bush as a troop of playing-card soldiers marched by, a fistful of leaves away. Then he heard the scrape of the principal's chair and watched her ghostly, pebbly figure come towards him and invite him in, invite him to sit down.

Tobias sat. Mrs. Armitage sat down, too, and thumbed through the story.

"Wilbur," she said. "From *Charlotte's Web*?"

Tobias nodded hesitantly. Sweet talk. She was going to engage him in conversation before she brought out the thumb screws.

"So how did Sergeant Steele end up with Wilbur and Winnie-the-Pooh and the others?" she asked. "Has he been raiding all the imaginary places?"

Tobias looked for the trap. "The zoo doesn't actually belong to Sergeant Steele," he said.

"Who does it belong to?"

Tobias scratched his head. "I don't know."

Mrs. Armitage frowned. "The writer must be sovereign over the worlds he creates," she said.

Tobias would have liked the chance to write that down. It sounded like a handy thing to know. But Mrs. Armitage was not finished.

She looked over her glasses at Tobias. "I think part of the problem here, Toby, is that Ms. Knieppe was hoping her students would recount events that had really happened to them this summer."

Tobias nodded. "I know," he said. "She heard me telling someone about wrestling with a tiger on my way to the cottage. She said it sounded really interesting and she hoped I would write about it." He didn't go on.

"And?" said Mrs. Armitage.

"And I tried," said Tobias. "But it wouldn't come."

"Tell me about it," said Mrs. Armitage, leaning back in her chair. She seemed to want to hear about wrestling the tiger. But Tobias shrugged and was silent.

"Did it really happen?"

"Yes," said Tobias.

"Then why don't you want to share it with me, with your classmates?"

Through Mrs. Armitage's window, Tobias could see the man in the uniform getting into his truck. The truck was silver and said *Mercury Messenger Service* on its side. There was a picture of a guy with wings on his heels running like a halfback with a package in his hands. The man in the uniform was whistling.

"Tobias?"

"I already told them!" said Tobias. "We were going to the cottage and we stopped to get gas and they had a tiger cub in a cage. The man at the gas station said I could go in the cage with him if I wanted, so I went in. It was cute. We wrestled a bit and my mom took a picture. I can show you the picture if you don't believe me."

"I do believe you," said Mrs. Armitage sincerely. "It sounds like a great story. Don't you think that's why Ms. Knieppe wanted you to write it down? Don't you feel that's why she was disappointed?"

Tobias watched the Mercury Messenger Service truck pull out of the school driveway onto Alta Vista Drive. He wondered where the next stop was and what all those packages contained.

Mrs. Armitage turned to see what Tobias was looking at, but the truck was already gone.

"She already knew the story," said Toby. "Everybody in class knew the story. It just wasn't worth writing it out."

"I see," said Mrs. Armitage, nodding. "So instead you decided to fire-bomb Wonderland."

"It was sort of a joke," said Tobias. "The class liked it."

"I'm sure they did," said Mrs. Armitage in a disapproving voice. The end of her sentence was like the bony end of a chicken drumstick. Mrs. Armitage bit down on the word and Tobias figured the sweet talk was over and the lecture was coming. But he was wrong again.

"It is funny," she said. "Tweedledum and Tweedledead, I mean. I'm not 'appalled' by it, Tobias, in case you're wondering. I think it is very imaginative."

"Thank you," said Tobias.

"Ms. Knieppe, however, is correct in thinking that the content of this story is inappropriate for the assignment, and I agree with her on that. But my guess is that you knew it was inappropriate and that's why you wrote it. Am I correct?"

Tobias shrugged.

"This was written purely for its shock value," said Mrs. Armitage.

"No," said Tobias. "It was fun."

Mrs. Armitage didn't look at the clock or anything, but she suddenly looked like someone who had a lot of other things to do and not a lot of time.

"I mean," said Tobias, "I wrote it for a laugh. That was part of it . . ."

"Yes?"

"And I guess I was a little mad, that was part of it . . ."

"Mad?"

"About having to write the tiger story."

"I see. And . . ."

"And . . ." Tobias stopped short as if at a chasm. Chased by the playing-card soldiers through a minefield, he was now at the brink of Dead Man's Leap. The enemy was right behind him and down below he could see the mangled bodies of kids who had tried to raid Wonderland before and failed. Where had it all gone wrong?

"And it just came to me," he said.

"It just came to you," said Mrs. Armitage.

It didn't seem much of an answer.

⸻

Peach was waiting for him after school. "Let me guess," she said. "You have to clean the gym floor with a toothbrush, right?"

"I wish!" said Tobias, falling in beside her. She waited for him to tell her. It wasn't that she actually stopped talking — Peach never stopped talking — but she didn't press him. She talked about a stamp her great-aunt had sent her from Guyana for the stamp collection her great-aunt seemed to think she had. And then she went on about how at her riding class the past Wednesday, Amelia, the girl who touched manta rays and spelled so well, had fallen off her pony.

"No way," said Tobias, grinning.

"Okay," said Peach. "She didn't fall, but she rode appallingly."

Then they talked about a bunch of appalling things until they were suddenly standing at Peach's driveway.

"So?" she said.

Tobias kicked at some fallen leaves. "I've got to write the tiger essay," he said.

"Is that all?" said Peach. "You got off easy."

Tobias looked at her. "I won't do it," he said. "I can't."

***

Tobias's mother was in the backyard putting her garden to bed. He gave her the news, all of it.

"Why won't you do it?" she said. "Is it a matter of principle or something?"

Tobias tried to think why he couldn't write the essay. "There's no surprise to it," he said.

"Well, this is a fine kettle of fish," said his mother.

She made him carry the lawn chairs to the garage and then help with dinner. She made him roll out the perogi dough while she read his story and the notes on it from Ms. Knieppe and Mrs. Armitage. His mother laughed at something, but Tobias wasn't sure if it was the story or the notes she was laughing at.

"Couldn't you talk to them?" he asked.

His mother patted him on the shoulder and shook her head. She started frying onions.

"I'm not doing it," said Tobias. His mother said nothing. Tobias rolled and rolled. His wrists ached. There is nothing tougher than perogi dough.

———

Peach phoned right after dinner. "You gonna do it?"

"Nope," said Tobias. "They can throw me to the tigers, as far as I'm concerned."

"But it's easy," said Peach. "You could write it with your eyes tied behind your back."

"I just can't make myself do it," said Tobias.

Peach was silent on the other end, but Tobias waited. Sometimes she was just hitching up her sock or reading the newspaper — her mother said she had very poor telephone manners — but Tobias was used to it. Sometimes she was thinking. That was what it was this time.

"Can you come over?" she said.

———

"What about your assignment?" said his mom. Tobias lied. He promised he would get right to it when he got back. Since he didn't say that he refused to do it, which is what he had said all through dinner, she let him go.

———

Peach was at her kitchen table writing on a pad of foolscap. An untouched piece of chocolate cake sat beside her. A dollop of ice cream melted by its side. Peach's mother cut a piece of cake for Tobias. Tobias sat down and watched. Peach kept writing.

"Your manners, young lady," said her mother, but she didn't go on about it and left the two of them alone in the silence of melting ice cream.

Finally Peach stopped writing. She sat up straight and held out the pad of paper in front of her to look it over.

"Exceptional," she whispered.

"What's going on?" said Tobias.

Peach said, "Are you absolutely sure you won't write the tiger story?"

Tobias gritted his teeth. He looked as if he was going to scream.

"Good," said Peach. "Because I've written it for you."

She handed him the foolscap pad.

The Summer of the Tiger
by Tobias Green

Every summer we go up to our cottage. I really look forward to swimming and waterskiing. Also my two cousins Terry and Dave live up there all year round and we do lots of things together like going to the antique boat show and fishing. But little did I know that this summer the best part of the trip was going to be the getting there!

"What?" said Tobias. "This is gross."

"No," said Peach. "It's appalling. And it gets worse."

So, while she helped herself to her much deserved piece of cake, Tobias read on.

We always stop at the Kritchmar Esso on our way north. There's an old pop bottle cooler there and Mom and Dad let us choose whatever soft drink we want. They also have a big cage out back of the old service station where there is sometimes an orphaned deer or bear cub. Once there was even an eagle which sat on this dead tree in the cage yelling at everybody. The Kritchmars just keep the animals for a week or two, then they let them go. Imagine our surprise when we arrived this time to find a real tiger cub!

"Imagine our surprise." Tobias wrinkled his nose. "It sounds just like Amelia's story about petting the manta rays."

"I'm glad you noticed," said Peach.

Tobias read on. He stopped and looked at Peach again. "How do you know all this stuff, anyway?"

Peach rolled her eyes. "I've heard the story about a hundred times," she said.

Tobias read in silence, shaking his head in disbelief. "She'll never believe I did this," he said when he had finished. "It's got A+ written all over it."

"That's the beauty of it," said Peach, finishing her cake and taking a forkful of Tobias's. "Ms. Knieppe thinks you are very creative. That's why she gets so disappointed with you. This will just prove to her that she was right all along. Teachers like that. Of course, you'll have to write it out again in your own ugly scrawl. And don't tell me you can't do it because it would be wrong or unethical or something. This isn't some sit-com. This is life or death."

Tobias pushed his own piece of cake towards Peach. "Thanks," he said. She took another forkful and pushed it back.

"It's going to cost more than a piece of cake," she said.

Tobias looked worried. Peach got up, left the room and ran upstairs. She came down a minute later with her hands behind her back.

"What?" said Tobias.

"You can have the A+ essay," she said, "but in return I want you to read this." Then, from behind her back, she brought out a copy of *Alice in Wonderland*.

Tobias grimaced.

"Read it," she said. She was about to hand him the book but instead she grabbed a tea towel and made him wipe his hands. The book was a beautiful edition with a clear plastic cover and gold lettering.

"What do you mean?"

Peach grabbed the book from him and opened it at random. "The-players-all-played-at-once-without-waiting-for-turns," she read. "They're called 'words,' Toby. *Read* them."

"But why?" said Tobias. "I know the story."

Peach sighed. "Well, then I guess you won't be needing this," she said. She picked up the foolscap essay and, rolling it up, she took it firmly in two fists and slowly started to tear.

"Hold it!" said Tobias. "Give me a chance to think!"

Peach waited. Tobias looked miserable. She looked away. Then she sighed again, unrolled the essay, smoothed it out and handed it to him. "Sorry," she said. "Jeez, I sounded just like Ms. Knieppe."

Tobias took the essay. Then he reached out and took the book, too.

"It's okay," said Peach. "I'm not going to make you read it."

"I'll read it," he said. "Really."

Peach's eyes lit up. "Tonight?" she asked.

"Tonight!"

"It's only 140 pages of big type and you don't have to read the last three or four pages where she wakes up, because that's garbage."

"Okay, okay!" said Tobias. "It's a deal."

Peach smiled triumphantly.

Tobias shook his head. "You're the worst best friend a guy ever had," he said.

He copied out her essay without changing a word. He wrote it in his best handwriting. Then, while his folks watched "Unsolved Mysteries," Tobias settled into the task of reading *Alice in Wonderland*. He knew Peach would quiz him on it and even though he remembered the movie, she would catch him out some way or other if he tried to fake it.

He read late. And he stayed up still later.

The next morning he showed Peach what he had done. "The Summer of the Tiger" was nicely bound with a cover made from torn strips of orange construction paper glued onto black. Very tigerish. There was a plastic dust jacket with gold lettering. It was pretty impressive. He also presented Peach with a little something he had written in his notebook.

"Tweedledum and Tweedledead: The Return." Peach looked dubious. She read it in silence.

The first paragraph showed no signs of improvement. Sergeant Steele and his Desperate Throng throttled the weasely counterspy, found the old map and dug out the rabbit hole just as they had done in the earlier version. They parachuted down the hole and gave themselves hypodermic needles full of Smallness just like before. But having blasted down the door — bazookas blazing — and entered the lovely garden, everything changed.

In the new version, the Desperate Throng couldn't find anybody to annihilate. Wonderland was deserted, or so it seemed. Then, suddenly, the whole deadly group was trapped. It was an elaborate trap, too, the best thing Tobias had ever thought of. They were led before her royal majesty the Queen of Hearts who rolled her eyes magnificently. "Sentence first — Verdict afterwards," roared the queen, and then, despite the protestations of Steele and company, her majesty roared again, "Off with their heads!" The next thing Sergeant Steele and his surly crew knew, they were all just little boys in short pants being kissed awake by a bunch of nice sisters at a picnic.

Peach loved it.

It was his gift to her, but Tobias borrowed it back right away. "Just for a minute," he promised.

In the office he persuaded Ms. Rowanook of the orange hair to make a copy of both stories for the principal. Tobias left them in her mailbox with a note explaining who had written what. He said in the note that he wasn't going to tell Ms. Knieppe about Peach writing the essay for him, but that if the principal needed to tell her, he would understand. As far as he could tell, Mrs. Armitage never did tell, either. Ms. Knieppe seemed altogether pleased with "The Summer of the Tiger." She said it was just what she was looking for.

She gave him a B+. After all, the assignment was a day late.

THE CLEARING

THE boy stopped at the top of You-and-Me-Pal Hill and kicked off his skis. He leaned against a rock. The sun was high and the glare on the snow hurt his eyes. He hurt everywhere. But at least he was outside again, moving through the windless day, his skis breaking a new trail.

He got his breath back. He couldn't shake the dizziness but he settled into the middle of it, found somewhere there that wasn't moving. Down the high meadow was Far-Enough Swamp, though he couldn't see it through the cedar and balsam that hugged the reedy shore.

"This is rich land," his dad had said once. "Where else you gonna find a swamp with a fir collar?"

The boy trained his eyes at a break in the trees. If this was a time-travel story, someone would come now. Maybe a Mohawk brave silently tracking a white-tail deer. He was ready. He would jump out at the deer and scare it — herd it — back into the path of the brave's arrow. It was a cold winter.

The brave would be thankful. He might take the boy back home to meet his dad and mom.

The boy watched and waited. Nothing.

Rich land — what a joke. Solid granite with a rind of dirt only Pollyanna could call soil. Farmers had once tried to cultivate this area. Snow-rounded pyramids of rocks along the cedar fence lines testified to their efforts; those and straggly apple orchards gone wild. But these meadows had been turned over to the hardier grasses — to juniper and thorn and prickly ash; to the fir trees that ringed Far-Enough Swamp.

The boy took a deep breath of bright, cold air. It was minus ten degrees Celsius, but he took off his gloves. They were wet inside with sweat, like the sheets of the bed he had left behind, clammy and constricting.

Where was his time-travel connection? In those stories the hero was always lonely, and he was lonely. The kid in a time-travel story was usually sick, too, and he was sick. For how long now, he didn't care to recall.

He started to shiver. Then he slipped back into his skis and shooshed down the meadow towards the gap in the trees that led to the swamp.

On the swamp there were many tracks: brush wolf and fox and rabbit. No humans. He followed the path of two wolves who seemed to be going more or less his way.

There was a wire fence property line right through the middle of the swamp. He climbed over it without taking off his skis. He imagined himself making an escape. He pushed himself hard, ducking invisible enemy fire, until the fence and his imaginary enemy were lost to view around a bend in the meandering waterway. Deeper and deeper he escaped into the silent forest, a graveyard of grey stumps and the spiny skeletons of trees.

He was trespassing now. This was Ken Axelrod's land and, after crossing the dyke, the Starkweathers, the Beresfords, the Strongs, the Frosts. But after that, he couldn't say anymore where he was. There were no signs of civilization out here and, in his dizziness, the sun was no help — it seemed lost itself. The only thing he knew for sure was that he was heading away, his sick bed slipping farther and farther behind.

At last he saw something in the distance that was not dead, not stumps. A hockey rink in a clearing. Rag-tag nets; sticks, broken or intact, stuck in the snow bank like a rickety fence; a bench carved out of ice with an old pine plank on top. A frozen toque.

Coming to the rink, the boy slipped out of his skis. He sat on the bench. He noticed the snow shovels. Suddenly, sick and tired as he was, an idea started ticking over in him.

There was three or four centimetres of fresh snow on the rink. The boy pushed at the snow with his foot; it flew up like so many feathers. He started to shovel. The joke of it flowed like fresh blood to his aching muscles. He shovelled like a boy possessed. He laughed a little to himself. He whistled.

Then, just as suddenly, he stopped. Looking up, he saw someone in the trees at the swamp's edge staring at him. He felt cold all over.

"Hey," the boy on the ridge called to him. "Hi."

Shaking, he dropped the shovel and ran for his skis. He fumbled with his binding. There was no such thing as time travel. There was only wishful thinking. This should not have happened.

The boy was coming. "It's all right," he cried.

But it wasn't all right. The intruder was stomping, sliding down the slope of the woods to the shoreline.

The skier turned himself towards home. His tips crossed and he fell over hard, then clambered to his feet again.

"Wait," the intruder cried. "Don't go."

But the skier pushed himself off, digging his ski pole tips through the downy snow into the ice itself. Heaving himself homeward, following his tracks.

"Hey, I can help," yelled the intruder, coming nearer, crossing the ice, slipping, recovering.

But the skier was off. The other boy would never catch him now.

"Come again," the intruder called after him.

———

Ben watched until the skier was out of sight. He took over shovelling where the other boy had left off, stopping often and staring out across the swamp. The sun was sitting low behind the hills, casting long blue shadows. Sometimes he fancied he saw the boy far off, a lean shadow disentangling itself from those of dead trees.

The wind picked up. Already the ski tracks were sifting over. Ben pushed the snow around in a desultory way. After a while he heard his father coming. He put his shoulder down and heaved snow manfully.

"Yowzers!" said his father, with enough surprise in his voice that Ben laughed inside. "Good work, Ben."

"Ah, it was nothing," said Ben, huffing it up a bit.

"Pretty industrious," said his father. Ben thanked him. Out of the corner of his eye he caught his father scratching his head. "I came to give you a hand."

Ben stopped, sucked in a bucketful of frosty air. "I can handle it, Dad," he said, leaning on his shovel.

His father waited a minute more while Ben went on shovelling.

"I'm sorry about the fight," said his father. Ben scraped his shovel over the ice.

"That's okay," he mumbled, without turning around.

"It's just that . . ." his father began, " . . . sometimes it's as if you didn't really move out here with us at all."

"That's dumb!" Ben wanted to shout. "Where am I? Back home in the city? What choice does a twelve-year-old have but to be wherever his parents take him!" But he didn't say a thing, because it would come out wrong and ungrateful and the argument would start all over again. And that would ruin the wonderful joke of this magically cleared rink.

After some more minutes his father said, "It'll be dark soon," and he headed back towards the woods, the path, the house. When he was out of sight, Ben surveyed what was left of the smooth blanket of snow on the ice and went to work with a vengeance. It was some creative shovelling he did. Then he went home hungry for supper and ready to make up properly.

In the snow still left on the rink, he had written

COME AGAIN

Before the school bus the next morning he ran down from the house to check. His message was mostly gone. The rink was clear, but it appeared to be the work of the wind.

———

Over the next few days it warmed up. Then it froze. Then it snowed a whole night. Then the sun shone hot. It was a winter spell set on killing a swamp skating rink. But Ben's father wasn't the kind of man who gave up on a pet project easily. He and Ben tried to keep the surface smooth, mostly for Ben's sisters. Ben liked hockey, but he hadn't really gotten to know anyone much since they'd moved to the valley and playing hockey by yourself was — well, you could only score the winning goal in the final game of the Stanley Cup so many times before the thrill wore off. But whether he used the rink or not, he and his father would come down, often in the chill of the night, and fill buckets with water from a hole to spread as best they could—"Smoother, Ben, smoother"—under the icy moon.

Ben would always have his eye open for the stranger. He would look up suddenly across the swamp.

"Did you hear that?" he would say.

"You're a jumpy customer," his father would answer, not listening long enough or hard enough, shaking his head and chuckling to himself.

Ben asked on the school bus who the kid might be. It gave him something to talk about.

The weather heated up unseasonably. The top of the rink in the clearing thawed, then froze again from the top down, leaving a sandwich of water between the new ice and the thick grey ice below.

That was the first time Ben saw the mayfly wrigglers. The water nymphs swam up through cracks in the thick ice and got themselves stuck in the watery sandwich. Having escaped from the winter dark at the bottom of the pond, they swam like crazy black writing in the sunlight. They were stuck there. They were not alone. Ben saw a black splotch under the new ice. He was just wondering how a puck had got there when the splotch moved.

"Look at this!" he cried.

"Bullfrog tadpole," said his dad. "It'll die there, unless it finds its way back down. Shouldn't have been so nosy."

Ben wanted to watch it, but the new ice wasn't very thick, and his father didn't want him to go through and wreck the surface. They went up for dinner with the tadpole, big as a puck, in Ben's head. It swam around just under his skull, wanting out.

That night the moon was full again. And whether it was the moon or the trapped tadpole or just life, Ben and his folks got into another fight.

Ben wasn't ever sure how these things happened. He was usually reading an Archie comic at the time or rearranging his baseball card collection. The argument was always over something he had said or hadn't done or had implied or had complained about.

In his room, with a slammed door separating him from the family, Ben opened his journal to the last page where he kept his fight record.

Mom	*Dad*
x x x x x x	x x x x x x x x

He added a new x to Mom's column. She was catching up to Dad. He could still hear her pounding about downstairs, her voice raised for him to hear, door or no door.

He never got hit, but the words were big and noisy, like God yelling at Moses: words that blew your ears off.

Reaching for his baseball dictionary, Ben flipped to "earned run average."

earned run average *n.* (ERA) A pitcher's statistics representing the average number of runs legitimately scored from his deliveries per full nine-inning game (27 outs).

He tried to figure out his earned fight average n. (EFA). Earned — how did you determine that? What was average? What made a fight legitimate? Did he ever win any?

Ben messed with his pen on some scrap paper while his heart turned around in his chest like a dog looking for some place to settle down. Then he started to draw: a guy sliding into second just under the ball; just under the sweeping hand of the second baseman. Safe. When spring started again, there would be baseball. If he could just make it through this endless winter to baseball . . .

He turned the pages in the journal to the entry he had written about the Phantom Shoveller. He had painted a little comic strip in watercolours. In the picture Ben cried after the shoveller, "Come back, come back, I've still got the driveway to do!" Now he noticed the date on the page. It had been the day of the last full moon.

His dad suddenly opened the door, and Ben slammed the journal shut. Later he wasn't quite sure why the apology he tried to make resulted in another yelling match and another slammed door. He sat on his bed for a long time, trying to figure out whether this was actually a new fight for which he should reward his father with an X, raising his EFA, or whether this was just the same fight he had been having with his mom and into which his dad had entered, kind of like a reliever in the late innings of a game.

Nobody came to kiss him goodnight. He didn't change into his pyjamas. He didn't turn out his light. He stomped, boiling mad, downstairs and made himself some toast just after his parents had put the girls to bed. He made several trips to the bathroom. In short, he gave them every opportunity to crab at him some more, so that he could stumble through a real apology. Then everyone could make up and get the whole thing out of the way, and he could get to sleep. Instead, they left him to stew in his own juices.

Finally he heard them in the bathroom preparing for bed. Surely now they would notice his light. The door was wide open.

They didn't. He heard them turn out their own lights without so much as looking in on him.

They were treating him as if he were gone. As if maybe they had left him back in the city.

Ben flicked out his own bedside light and sat, arms crossed tight on his chest, breathing heavily in the dark. But it was not really dark; there was a full moon. It was almost bright enough to read by. Bright enough to leave by.

He was as quiet as a mouse until he was out of the house and then he slammed the door good and loud. Just one more slammed door in a night of slammed doors.

He was halfway to the clearing before he realized where he was heading. He had never been out in the woods so late—not alone, at least. Once the family had skated under the full moon with a bunch of neighbours, and even his sisters had stayed up until almost midnight. But on that occasion the bright night had been filled with chatter and hot chocolate, and he had not heard the noise the night makes all on its own. In the dead of winter, that noise is Silence.

Silence was something he had never heard in the city. It was a Silence to fill the wildness of the eastern forest; a silence as tall as the pines, as wide and as deep as the swampland. It filled him with an urgent longing.

He stood among the trees on the shore looking out at the shining rink. He waited for his father to come tromping through the brush after him. "Ben, Ben, this is ridiculous!" Then he could hurl himself at his father's chest and into his arms. But his father didn't come, and the Silence grew around him.

Then, because he had to do something to occupy his runaway mind, he slithered down the snowy bank to the swamp and walked quickly out across the clearing to the rink. There was a wind out there he had not felt in the shelter of the trees. It was a sound, anyway, almost soothing.

It took some time to locate the huge tadpole. On his knees to better spread out his weight, Ben watched it for several moments fearing that it was already dead, perhaps frozen into place, for the night had turned cold. Then it moved, squirming slowly but too stupid cold to look for the hole through which it had slipped into this place between places.

"Yes!" said Ben, and in a flash he was on his feet again and searching for his father's axe. He brought the axe down hard on the new ice — once, twice, three times—before finally cracking it. That woke the tadpole up!

"It's for your own good," said Ben.

The tadpole didn't swim far. It was trapped every which way, in the last pool of unfrozen water, a pool no more than a metre in diameter.

Ben whacked some more. Each whack sounded like a gunshot. Finally, with one last, mighty swing —Splat!—water sprayed up at him. He had broken through. He chipped away the chunks of surface ice, brought over the coffee can that his father used as a small bucket, and attempted to catch the frantic prisoner. He had made several dives at it, and his cuffs were getting pretty wet, when someone spoke.

"You gonna destroy the whole rink?"

For one wild, midnight second, Ben thought it was the tadpole. Then he swung around so fast that the bottom half of him slid into the pond.

There, just behind him, stood the phantom skier.

"The rink," said the boy. "You destroying it?"

"No," said Ben. "There's this tadpole." He clambered up, shaking his cold, damp leg to get some of the water off it. The boy approached him cautiously. Ben backed off a little. The boy bent down and looked into the hole. Ben saw the sweat stand out on his cheek and forehead, saw that he was shivering badly.

The stranger bent down. "Can you catch him?" he said.

Ben dropped to his wet knees beside the boy and picked up the coffee can. The stranger leaned back on his haunches, watching as Ben lowered the can into the shallow icy pond, quite suddenly an expert at the moonlight capturing of trapped tadpoles. In one deft swoop he swooshed the can out of the pond, triumphant. The two boys peered into it together and then ventured to look at each other.

"Come on," said Ben. He led the other boy to the hole his father kept open at the edge of the rink in order to draw water from the swamp below. It was covered with a bucket. "Here you go," said Ben, emptying the can into the hole. With a flip of its tail the creature was gone. The two boys watched the darkness for a moment.

"In a cartoon," said Ben, "the tadpole would come to the surface and wink or something."

"Or there would be a bubble," said the boy, "and when you popped it the word 'thanks' would come floating out."

They smiled at each other. It was only a fleeting smile. Each of them had things on his mind. The stranger looked back to the axe hole in the rink.

"I'll have some explaining to do," said Ben. "But I think my dad will understand."

"You took some initiative," said the boy, the tail of a smile reappearing on his pale face.

"Right," said Ben. "I was industrious." They both laughed. Then, because he couldn't hold it any longer, Ben said, "Who are you?"

It was exactly the wrong thing to say. The boy's face seemed troubled again. He looked back at the hole in the rink and then at the open hole in front of them and then all around, as if he was looking for something, some way to explain.

"I didn't mean to be rude," said Ben. But it was already too late. The boy stood up, tall and thin— too thin. Head down, he went for his skis. "Wait," said Ben, desperate now, for he was losing people all over the place tonight.

"I can't stay," said the boy.

"Then I'll come with you," said Ben, following him, staying close enough to touch the boy's elbow.

"You can't," said the boy, pulling his arm out of reach. He clipped on his skis.

"Why not?" said Ben.

The boy was breathing hard. He started moving, finding his tracks in the snow. "You won't be able to keep up," he called over his shoulder.

Ben started after the boy on foot. "Just watch me," he shouted, breaking into a tight and cautious run. "I can't go home. Wait up."

Across the moonlit swamp he pursued the skier, falling farther and farther behind. "I'll get lost," he yelled. "And it'll be your fault!"

"Go home," the boy called back at him.

It started to snow, one more curtain between Ben and home and between Ben and the boy, now almost out of sight. But Ben wasn't going to let go of him. He followed the tracks. How hard it was to move on this land without skis. His legs were city legs: pavement hard and strong, but he could not keep his footing on the snow-covered swamp. He would break through the crust here, slip out on the ice there. But he kept going.

At one point the ski trail joined up with the tracks of a pair of coyotes — brush wolves they called them around here. Ben faltered in his stride.

"Please!" he called out across the swamp. "I don't want to be somebody's dinner."

"Go home."

Then, finally, the tracks came to a fence, and not far beyond that headed towards the shoreline, the woods. In the fringe of trees there was no wind and Ben paused for a moment to catch his breath. He looked back across the swamp. The snow fell quietly. Already it had laid fine tissue in his footsteps. How much longer would there be a path to follow home?

Then, behind him, back in the direction he had come from, the coyotes howled. It was a mad yip, yip, yipping. The sound zinged through him. He was not the only crazy one on the prowl tonight. It was the moon they wanted, not him, he told himself, but the sound was enough to send him quickly on his way, after the boy.

At the top of the meadow he stopped at a rocky outcropping. Looking down the other side, he thought he saw a striding shadow slip into the woods. "Yes!" He tore off in pursuit. Sinking into the deep drifts of the meadow, scratching himself in the prickly ash, pressed on by the baying coyotes, following tracks that grew fainter and fainter under the snow-beclouded moon.

He emerged at last from an old logging road at a small, neat cottage with the lights still on. It was like something from a fairy tale, with him as the miserable, poor straggler. Unable to move another step, breathing heavily, soaked with sweat and numb where the icy water of his tadpole rescue mission had soaked through his jeans, he leaned against a tree. He caught his breath and watched the uncurtained windows of the cottage. He could make out a woman reading by a fire. No one else.

Ben gathered up what was left of his shredded courage and marched up to the door. When he was close enough, he checked the walls to make sure they were not gingerbread.

He had no idea what he was going to say. His mind was muzzy with the cold and a buzzing tiredness of limb and spirit he had never experienced before. He would have to say something, he told himself, and though words would not form in his head, he knocked again and again. Then the woman was at the door, opening it in a hurry, keeping back a barking, slathering golden retriever with her foot, and all Ben could think to say was "I'd like to phone my mom, please."

She took him in. The dog bounced on him. A man appeared in his undershirt and cleared a place by the fire. Tea came, and blankets. The man made a joke about what Ben's chattering teeth were saying in Morse code, and by then Ben could actually laugh a little, though he had no right to laugh or even to be alive, he reckoned, all things considered. He told them about the coyotes. They had heard them, too.

The woman got his phone number and talked to his mom. She turned to him. "She's on her way."

Then Ben asked if a boy lived there.

"No," said the woman, shaking her head. "A daughter off at college. No boy." So he didn't tell them about the skier.

It was Ben's dad who came because the coyotes had woken up both the girls with full-moon nightmares, and Mom was feeding them full-moon carrot cake and hot milk.

"So you'll be coming home to a party," his father said, squeezing him tightly. No one asked any questions. Ben didn't try to explain. Dad had met the couple, the Robbs, at some valley shindig. He couldn't thank them enough.

"Ah, heck," said Mr. Robb. "It kind of livens up a dull evening." And then it was time for Ben to change into the warm clothes his father had brought along and head home.

At the front door, Ben noticed a pair of skis. They were leaning in the corner of the mud room. They were just like the ones the boy had worn. But they weren't wet at all. The woman noticed him looking at them, and she got a frown on her face, which made Ben feel bad. He concentrated on putting on his boots. His hands were shaking badly.

They were climbing into the car and Dad was tucking him into the passenger seat like a little kid when the door of the cottage reopened and Mrs. Robb called out to Ben's father. He closed Ben's door and went back to the house. Ben watched them talking through the oval window of the front door. Then, amazed, he saw the woman handing the red skis to his father. Meanwhile, Mr. Robb opened a closet and emerged with ski boots and poles. Then it was goodbye all over again and Dad was making his way to the car laden down with this mysterious treasure. The skis wouldn't fit in the trunk so they had to be shoved into the back seat with the tips hanging over Ben's shoulder.

"They're for you," said his father with a catch in his voice. "Make getting around out here a whole lot easier." He didn't say anything about running away.

And he didn't say any more just then. Ben looked at him in the dashboard light and saw that he was choked up about something.

"It was the last thing they had left of their own son," his father said at last. There was a long pause. Snow fell. Ben kept his eyes on the road.

"It's been five years."

They turned onto a now familiar road.

"He was your age."

Neighbours' mailboxes glided by: the Beresfords, Strongs, Frosts.

"They wanted me to thank you."

Thank him? Ben was puzzled. They pulled into the driveway and stopped the car and had a big shaky hug together. Over his father's shoulder, Ben could see his mom in the kitchen, the girls sitting in their nighties. He wanted to get in and be a part of it.

Ben and his dad climbed out of the car wrestling the skis out with them.

"They just couldn't seem to let him go," said his father.

And far away the coyotes started yip, yip, yipping at the moon.

SOME OF THE
KINDER PLANETS

USUALLY when Quin stayed at her grand-mother's apartment in the city, she got to sleep in the big bedroom, and her grandmother slept in the closet. It was actually a storage room, but Nanny Vi liked to say she was "sleeping in the closet these days" just to get a rise out of people. Quin's brother, Mark, shivered at the very thought of sleeping in the closet, which was just big enough for a bed, a bedside table and some shelves. But Quin loved the little windowless room. She called it the dollhouse, because it was all got up pretty with a lacy-edged lampshade and embroidered cushions. It was like the tiny room of a princess: a room in a tower, maybe. Without a window, it could be anywhere.

So Quin was excited to learn that on this trip, *she* was going to be sleeping there. She was going to be staying in the city a long time, and while Nanny Vi didn't mind giving up her bedroom for a weekend visit, she wasn't sure about three months in the closet.

Three months away from home. Maybe longer if the play was held over. Three months in Toronto. There was talk about the show going to New York. The idea buzzed inside Quin's head like a fly in one of Nanny Vi's gold and blue tea cups. She would miss her best friend, Sarah. Her parents and Mark would come down to visit. But she would have Nanny Vi all to herself. Nanny Vi was going to be home-schooling Quin while she was in the city.

The play was called *Some of the Kinder Planets*. It wasn't a children's play, either. Quin got to play the part of Thea. She had a lot of lines. She even got to die in the second act. It was very exciting.

She got the part through a series of coincidences which, if you read about them in a novel, you wouldn't believe.

Here's what happened. The church choir from her home town sang at the cathedral in Toronto. A friend of the choirmaster's was a theatrical agent, and when he was introduced to Quin after the show, he said, "Thea!" right out loud and insisted that she read for the part. He managed to get her an audition. Out of 350 kids who tried out, Quin got the role. It all happened very fast.

"Weren't you nervous?" Sarah asked her.

"There wasn't time to be," Quin said. But the strange thing is, she hadn't been nervous at all.

Before then she had only ever been in productions of *Oliver* and *Annie* at her school. Suddenly she was living in Toronto and making $521.71 a week. The Royal Alex was what they called an "A" house. The tops. And Nanny Vi was to be her "companion." They would travel to rehearsals by taxi.

Quin loved rehearsals. There was a famous British actress in the cast and Quin couldn't take her eyes off her. But for the first few days, being at her grandmother's apartment on the seventeenth floor was the most exciting part of the adventure. From the balcony she could see Lake Ontario, while below her, Toronto spread out as far as she could see in every other direction. She imagined all the places they would go; places they never had time to see when the family came for weekend visits. And movies! There was no movie theatre in Quin's home town. At Nanny Vi's she could watch about three thousand TV stations whenever she wanted, as long as it wasn't too late. Her grandmother liked to eat all over the place, sometimes standing up at the counter in the kitchen. Sometimes they ate out: in Chinatown or at a deli.

Nanny Vi woke Quin every morning with a cup of hot sugary tea—"fairy tea," she called it—paled with warm milk. Unless it snowed. If it snowed, Nanny Vi brought Quin hot chocolate.

"When the crocuses come up, I'll bring you a Coke float," said Nanny Vi. So even though Quin slept in a windowless room, she always knew what kind of a day it was when she woke up. At the apartment, even getting up was exciting. The bathroom was carpeted and warm. At home, her parents kept the house at "a good healthy" 18 degrees Celsius. Over breakfast, Nanny Vi listened to a noisy radio program with lots of chatter and laughing about the weather. At home, her parents listened to CBC Stereo, which only ever seemed to play Mozart. Sometimes Quin and Nanny Vi had left-over spaghetti for breakfast.

———

Nanny Vi talked in her sleep. When Quin phoned home, she told Mark.

"Didn't you know about that?" he said. "It's really freaky."

The first time it happened, Quin woke up and had no idea where she was. But there was a night-light in the hall, and her door was never closed. She heard the noise again. She thought there was a stranger in the apartment. She lay in bed not breathing and listened. The voice was low and gravelly.

When the voice came no closer, she slipped out of bed and cautiously made her way to the door. She could tell the voice was coming from Nanny Vi's room, and she wondered who could possibly be visiting at such a late hour. She thought about getting the hammer from the kitchen. The voice sounded like it belonged to the kind of person you'd want to hit with a hammer. Then, gradually, she realized that the voice was a sleeping voice, a dreaming voice.

"Your head is so full of bath accessories, they're coming out your volcano tap-water lips," growled Nanny Vi. Could it possibly be her? By now Quin was wide awake; she stifled a giggle. Nanny Vi growled again. "Get out, get out, you snotty-nosed lesser frigate-bird!"

Quin stood silently at Nanny Vi's bedroom door. In the darkness she saw the comfortable lump under the bedclothes, unmistakably her grandmother.

"Out, I say!" growled the lump. Quin could only think how funny it would be to tell Mark.

"What can that all be about?" said Nanny Vi in the morning, when Quin told her about her sleep talk.

"I don't know," said Quin. "What's a lesser frigate-bird?"

Her grandmother had no idea, but she looked it up in her bird book. "Huh!" she said. "It's smaller than the magnificent frigate-bird, that's what it is." She shook her head as she showed Quin the picture. "Now, finish your cereal. The taxi's waiting."

In the taxi, Quin said, "You sounded like the troll under the bridge in the three billy goats gruff." They both laughed at that. Nanny Vi a troll!

It was around then that the rehearsals got harder for Quin. That night as she and Nanny Vi sat on the bed with trays and ate dinner watching Wheel of Fortune, Quin said, "I'm having trouble with dying."

"I know the feeling," said Nanny Vi. She laughed, and everybody on Wheel of Fortune clapped loudly. The comment made Quin feel uncomfortable. When Wheel of Fortune was over they ate pound cake in the living room, the city glittering and growling seventeen floors below.

"The director wants me to think of something terrifying so that Thea looks right for her death scene," said Quin.

Nanny Vi thought for a bit. "How about a magnificent frigate-bird?" she said. "*Hyah, hyah, hyah!*" she squawked, flapping her arms. Quin practised looking terrified. It didn't really work.

In her nightie before bed she looked in the mirror in the bathroom. She remembered seeing *The Watcher in the Woods* on television with Sarah. Sarah had been terrified. Remembering how Sarah had looked, Quin opened her eyes wide and clenched her teeth. But she only looked like she was pulling a face. The director had said, "No face-pulling, dear."

Nanny Vi didn't usually stay for rehearsals. She found them boring. The next day when she arrived to pick up Quin, the director, Keith, came to talk to her.

"This grandchild of yours is far too well adjusted," he said. Quin laughed a little nervously. It had been a difficult afternoon. Keith smiled thinly. "Doesn't anything scare her?" he asked.

Nanny Vi looked at Quin. "Hmmmm," she said. "I'll see what I can dream up."

In the taxi she said, "That director would be enough to scare *me*." It was meant to be a joke. Quin didn't say anything. She crossed her arms on her chest and looked out at the city flying by. It didn't seem very glamorous at street level, but it hardly mattered. She wasn't going to have much time to explore anyway.

Nanny Vi patted her on the arm and redirected the taxi-driver to a pizza place she knew. They got a large to go. "So there's some left over for breakfast," said Nanny Vi. "Maybe we should get anchovies."

Quin screwed up her face. Her grandmother laughed. "Just trying to scare you," she said.

"Gross isn't scary," said Quin.

They walked home through the gathering dark, through a cold November rain, through a park of suspicious pigeons and nosy seagulls.

"Scat, you ruffians," said Nanny Vi, swinging her umbrella at them. Then, suddenly, she said to Quin, "The creeps! That's what you need. The creeps!"

At home, while Quin made up trays for dinner, Nanny Vi searched through her bookshelves. "I know it's here somewhere," she said. "Aha!"

She brought to the living room an old copy of Grimm's fairy tales.

"The Boy Who Went Out Into the World to Learn What Fear Was," she read. "This ought to do the trick." Quin munched on her pizza while Nanny Vi read between mouthfuls.

The story was about a simpleton who wasn't afraid of anything. He was jealous of his older brother who got the creeps if he walked past the graveyard at night or heard a spooky tale by the fireside. "It gives me the creeps!" the older boy cried. The younger boy, sitting on his stool in the corner, only sighed. "I wish I could learn how to get the creeps."

His father kicked the simpleton out of the house. In vain he tried to get the creeps. But ghosts and dead men on the gallows and ghouls and vicious black cats and malevolent magic beds had no effect on him. Three nights in a haunted castle had no effect on his poor simple mind. But by staying there for those three nights, the boy was able to rid the haunted castle of its curse, and for his bravery the grateful king gave him his gorgeous daughter's hand in marriage.

"Ooh, that's pretty creepy," said Quin.

"Getting a gorgeous daughter is creepy?"

"No. It just says he got her hand!"

The simpleton was smart enough to appreciate marrying the beautiful princess, but he still wished he knew what the creeps were. The princess's chambermaid knew just what to do. That night while he was sleeping, she went to the brook that ran through the castle garden and fetched a bucket full of minnows. Making her way up to the newly-weds' bed chamber, she pulled back the sheets and poured the icy water and minnows over the simpleton. The little fish flapped all over him, causing him to wake up and exclaim, "Oh, I've got the creeps! I've got the creeps! Now I know, dear wife, just what the creeps are."

The end.

Nanny Vi thumped the book shut and glared at her granddaughter like a sorceress. "Scared, my pretty?" she asked. There was some of her gravelly dream voice in the wicked-witch imitation.

Quin glared back. "Don't get any ideas," she said.

Nanny Vi re-opened the book just a crack and, reaching into it, came out with an imaginary minnow wriggling in her fingers, *flap, flap, flap*. She dangled it in front of Quin's face and then tried to plop it down Quin's shirt. They laughed their heads off.

———

That night Quin lay in bed in the close darkness of the closet dollhouse, her head cradled in her arms. She tried to think of scary things. She tried to imagine her parents dying. She couldn't. But the trying made her sad. The director didn't want *sad*.

Then she recalled one night when there was a storm and her parents weren't home. There was a power failure and Quin went to get a flashlight from the kitchen. She and Mark had been watching TV and Mark waited in the TV room. Suddenly she heard him yelling. "There's people outside!" he shouted. His voice was panicky. "They're surrounding the house!" Quin hurried back to him. And sure enough, there were lights in the woods, flashing here and then there, on and off. Fireflies.

"They're fireflies," she said. After that Mark just sat in the dark and let it sink in: fireflies. He was two years older than Quin but he was nervous, imaginative. He also liked to watch scary movies. Quin had no interest in them.

Now, lying in her windowless room seventeen floors above the busy night streets of Toronto, Quin tried to feel Mark's fear of that moment. Hunters in the woods. No creeps came to her.

"Maybe I just don't have any imagination," she thought. She rolled over to face the wall.

She thought of Thea, sickly and living in a troubled, war-torn land. She thought of Thea's last scene, in an abandoned mansion with her Aunt Constance.

Constance is waiting for the phone to ring, not knowing if the rebels have cut the telephone lines. Thea is standing by a shattered window when suddenly the light breaks through the overcast and pours into the grey room. In the bright wedge of sunlight, she seems to see every particle of dust.

THEA: Is it true that there are creatures who live on dust?

CONSTANCE: Dustmites. Yes. Why?

THEA: Is there one dustmite per dust particle?

CONSTANCE: What? I don't know. Yes. How could there be room for more than one. Lie down, Thea. Stop fretting so.

THEA: It makes me think of the Little Prince. On his planet, you know. He has a flower.

(There is gunfire. Constance ducks. Thea doesn't move. Constance crawls to her.)

CONSTANCE: Get down, girl! They'll see you in the light! (She drags Thea down to the floor. Cradles her. Watches the phone.) Oh, why don't they phone! It's not so far.

THEA: Oh, it's very far ... I forget ... the flower. What is it, Aunt Constance?

(Constance has discovered blood on her dress. Thea's blood; she has been shot.)

CONSTANCE: Blood?

THEA: No ... a rose ... that's it ...

CONSTANCE: Thea!

THEA: And the baobobs ... the bad seeds ... they get so big ... Constance, their roots will shatter the little planet ... Constance? As soon as they are big enough to distinguish from the roses, the Little Prince has to ... dig ... them ... up ...

(Thea dies. There is more gunfire. Constance carries her out of the room.)

—————

The play goes on and on, and Quin, off stage, enjoyed watching the adults wrecking things and sorting things out and wrecking things all over again. When she first read the scene, Quin thought that dying in a play would be great. But Keith wanted her to "see" something fearful in her last moment. He wanted her to have an Image, he said — an Image she could look at in her mind's eye that terrified her from deep inside.

Quin rolled over in her bed to face the door. It was open; the night-light in the hall made the broadloom glow. Keith had brought in a magazine with an article about dustmites. The pictures, enlarged eight hundred times, made the mite look like a monster — an overweight crab. Quin had scrinched up her face. "Its legs look like asparagus," she had said.

"And to think they're everywhere." Keith had looked hopeful. "Frightening, eh?"

Quin had only nodded, disgustedly. "Yes," she had said. "I hate asparagus."

Now she tried to imagine monstrous dustmites with asparagus legs traipsing across the glowing landscape of the apartment broadloom. She closed her eyes and she could see a dustmite there, but it didn't look terrifying. Hardly. She could even imagine it as a pet: "Here, Fluffball. Roll over. Play dead."

Suddenly she heard Nanny Vi start to groan. She cocked her head to listen. Nanny Vi's troll voice rumbled down the hall.

"Nasty bushwhacking piece of work," she growled. "Lord, if my hair was on fire, I'd show you a thing or two!"

Weird.

But not scary.

The next day was Friday, the end of the second week of rehearsals. There was only one more week before *Some of the Kinder Planets* opened. Already Quin knew of four radio, newspaper and television interviews she would be doing next week, apart from the heavy rehearsal schedule. At the end of the first week of rehearsals, she had been sad at the prospect of the weekend. But today she looked forward to some time off.

Nanny Vi had a rummage sale that day. Her women's group was raising money for the Somalian refugees. "Now that's pretty scary stuff," she said, pointing to a picture in one of the Relief Fund's brochures. "Machine-gun-carrying soldiers killing innocent women and children and stealing food from them." As the taxi stalled in an early morning traffic jam, Quin read the brochure.

Was this scary? It seemed so far away. It made her heart hurt inside; it made her *angry*. Was this what Keith wanted?

Quin was just about to hand the brochure back when she read the part about sending donations. She shuddered with excitement.

"This is fabulous!" she said.

"It is?" said Nanny Vi.

"I've never sent any money to a charity in my life," said Quin. "Now I could. I could send a hundred dollars, even."

Nanny Vi looked thoughtful. "Yes," she said. "You could."

Quin settled back in her seat with a smile on her face, as the cab shot through a gap in the traffic and sped her towards the heart of downtown. It was only as Nanny Vi walked her into the Royal Alex towards the rehearsal studio that Quin felt a sinking feeling down in her stomach.

In all this wonderfulness, where was she to find scared?

"Well?"

Nanny Vi was there again. The rummage sale had been a massive success. She and Quin were sitting in a booth at a bar near the theatre having a TGIF—Thank God It's Friday—hot fudge sundae. It was Quin's turn to talk about *her* day.

"We stayed away from my death scene," said Quin, pressing the peanuts down into the ice cream.

"Is that good?" asked Nanny Vi.

Quin shrugged. "Keith said we'd give it a rest."

A klatch of noisy office people pushed through the double doors of the bar, laughing and clapping each other on the back. They sounded to Quin like the happy-go-lucky crew on the radio station Nanny Vi listened to in the morning.

"The famous actress talked to me," said Quin. "Behind Keith's back."

"Oh?" Nanny Vi's spoon paused halfway to her mouth. Chocolate in a thin stream dripped back into the sundae bowl.

"She said it was every child's right to live without fear: to live fearlessly. That's how she put it."

"Bravo!" said Nanny Vi.

"She did *Some of the Kinder Planets* when it ran in London. For two years. Can you imagine? And she said she'd been watching me and I was perfect for Thea."

Quin took a deep breath, an ice-cream-cold breath. "She said that instead of Fear, I should play the scene with Wonder. She said Keith will think it is Fear and he'll love it."

Nanny Vi put down her spoon and smiled a very satisfied smile. Quin smiled back.

"She said most adults don't know the difference anyway."

Her grandmother looked as if she was going to crack up. "I like this woman," she said.

Quin agreed. "There's only one problem," she said. "How do I play Wonder?"

———

Later that evening Quin and Nanny Vi curled up

with a bowl of popcorn and watched *The Wizard of Oz* on TV. It was one of Quin's favourite movies, but she couldn't concentrate. Her mind kept wandering.

Fear. Wonder. How did a person pretend these things? How had she ever got this part? She was no actor. An actor had to have an imagination, be able to see things that weren't there — see something that transformed her so that she looked different. Keith had said, "No face-pulling, dear." But what was an expression but face-pulling?

"Here's my favourite part," said Nanny Vi.

On the screen, Dorothy was sure pulling face. She was trapped on the ramparts of the wicked witch's castle. The soldiers were closing in. Nanny Vi grabbed Quin's hand and held it tightly. Then Dorothy got mad and threw water at the witch, and the witch began to melt.

"See!" said Nanny Vi. "Water again. Fearful stuff, with or without the minnows."

Quin laughed, but not very convincingly. Her grandmother squeezed her hand. "You're thinking too hard," she said.

"I know," snapped Quin. "So how do I stop thinking?"

She had never spoken to Nanny Vi like that before. Her chest felt all tight. She felt as if she had a popcorn kernel caught in her throat. She wanted to run to her little windowless dollhouse room and close the door. But she didn't budge.

They watched the end of the movie in silence. Then Nanny Vi pushed the Off button on the remote control, and the movie fizzled.

"How about some hot chocolate?" she said.

"I'm sorry," said Quin.

Nanny Vi patted her on the leg, but didn't say any more. She got up and left the room. Quin listened to her pottering in the kitchen. She picked up the remote control and turned the TV back on. "Tune in next Friday for another classic oldie," said a TV voice. And now on the screen Sinbad the Sailor held up his hands in major face-pulling fright as a towering lizard pounded down the beach towards him.

Quin punched the Off button. She would never find out what happened to Sinbad, she thought. Next Friday was opening night.

———◆———

And then, somehow, it was Friday. For Quin it was a frantic week filled with interviews and extra rehearsals. It was a week of encouraging winks from the leading lady and patient smiles from Keith. He didn't bug Quin about her death scene anymore. Instead, he brought her a lovely illustrated leather-bound copy of *The Little Prince*. Quin had read the book before — it made her fall asleep — but she appreciated the thought.

It was also a week filled with Nanny Vi talking in her sleep. She was so nervous. Not Quin.

Friday came, and with it, Quin's parents and Mark and Sarah, too. Sarah gave Quin an opening-night present of a pair of earrings. The tiny silver masks of comedy and tragedy. Her family gave her a huge box of flowers.

But the best thing of all came from Nanny Vi. Somewhere, she had found an old coloured print of a magnificent frigate-bird, which she had framed. The bird was flying on huge black wings with a jellyfish in its beak. And, although it might not have been her grandmother's idea, it was that picture that came suddenly swimming into Quin's mind in Act Two's tragic conclusion. She didn't actually see the magnificent frigate-bird in her mind's eye. She became it.

Fearlessly, she sailed out of her Aunt Constance's arms, over the packed electric darkness of the Royal Alex Theatre, through the doors and out into the night until she was soaring at last over the grey-green waters of the Gulf of Mexico.

STAR-TAKER

IT was August, 1867. Upper Canada had only been Ontario for a little over a month, a province in a new country. Edward George Lee had heard something about the talks in Charlottetown and wondered what it would mean being a Canadian, if it would be any different. It certainly wasn't going to stop Father from giving him chores.

On that day they were going to be clearing some forest up by Green Lake. Mixed hardwood and pine. And mosquitoes. Still, work was work and as his mama said with the old country purring in her voice, "Don't look a gift-horse in the mouth, Edward George."

So he was up at the whip-crack of dawn harnessing Buck and Brin and glad to be near their dusty oxen warmth, for the mornings were already as cool as the bite of a McIntosh apple. He had no idea that at fourteen years old he was going to become famous — famous and forgotten — all on that same August day.

They walked in silence. In this new country called Canada, would his father talk more than he was accustomed to? Eddie doubted it. He knew what the man was thinking anyway: that this job would finally afford him a new addition to the barn. It was all his father thought about these days.

A white-throated sparrow whistled its quavering three-note song. Eddie puckered up and joined in; the bird always answered back. More conversation than he'd hear all morning.

———

Captain Overman of the Ottawa Forwarding Company had hired Eddie's father to clear some land. The captain operated the steamboat *Jason Gould* up on Muskrat Lake. Papa was making three dollars a day, good money. And at the end of it, there would be something for Eddie. Father would present him with a crisp new three-dollar bill issued by the Colonial Bank of Canada.

The sun came up hard that morning. His papa did the axe work. Eddie's job was to hitch up the oxen team to the felled trees and draw them to the burn site. It was good timber they were burning, but there was good timber everywhere in this corner of the country.

"More timber than you could shake a stick at," Mama liked to say. All that forest—it gave her the willies. Eddie couldn't have imagined a time when there would not be endless forest everywhere. It was all he knew.

The smoke from the fire kept the mosquitoes and black flies at bay. But Eddie's eyes smarted, and the sweat boiled on the back of his neck. He took off his shirt, spread it out over the alder brush by the stream that meandered down to the lake.

Noon rolled around, as it will even on days when a person is about to become famous and forgotten. Father brought down a giant red pine. How it thundered as it hit the ground. It was around then that he sent Eddie home for his dinner. He left his father hacking that pine into sections. It was too big for the oxen to drag away as it was. Eddie was told not to dawdle. Father would be waiting for his own meal, which Eddie would carry back to him in the old biscuit tin.

It was good to escape the smoke and fire and walk down the concession trail out to the road. Stretch his legs, feel his spine unwind a bit. Let the sun turn his bare back as red hot as a cast iron pan. Mama kidded him about that when he arrived home, poking him with her finger and drawing it back as if it were sizzling.

"Lie down on the table, Eddie. I'll just mix up a batter of griddle cakes," said Mama. "Shame not to use a good iron nicely heated." Little Isabel laughed. She climbed up on Eddie's knee and rode to Banbury Cross while Mama cooked up a half dozen sausages.

When Eddie got back to Lot 12, Father was grateful for the break. He took the tin over to a stump where he could look out over the lake. Eddie stood by him for just a moment, watching a blue heron stalk the shore with her improbable long legs. She caught herself a fat bullfrog. Father wiped the grease off his cheek with a hunk of fresh bread, slapped another fat sausage in it, took a big bite.

Eddie drew away two of the logs, the lower portions of the huge red pine. But the third section just below the branches was not chopped clean. He had to pull it around sideways to break it off.

He dug away the moss and marl that the old tree lay in so he could get the chain around the log.

"Hiaiye!" he called out, slapping Buck on his sooty side. "Hiaiye!"

Smack. The oxen heaved their mighty shoulders and swung the log around. Eddie jumped back out of their path, ducking as branches swung past his head. And the log rolled back the moss like a blanket to reveal a bed of dark soil, which is where it lay, as if sleeping.

A round yellow thing no more than six inches in diameter.

———◆———

Fifty-two years later, Edward George Lee would visit the site with an historian fellow and show him just where it all happened. Not so limber anymore at sixty-six, he would duck and dance out of the oxen's way, acting out the whole little drama. He would tell the historian that the thing was ten inches across. Funny, how things grow in the memory . . .

———◆———

Fourteen-year-old Eddie picked the round thing up, flicked off the dirt, a curling brown centipede or two. With a grimy thumbnail he cleaned the groove that ran around the edge. There were all kinds of markings, figures cut into the metal, and there was an arm across it, pointed at one end and blunt at the other. With an effort he could move that arm a notch or two. It made him think of a compass.

Eddie had never heard of a navigational instrument called an astrolabe. He had never been away from these woods or anywhere near a sea, though one time he had watched a steamboat out on the Ottawa River chugging south-east towards Bytown. The Ottawa joined up with the St. Lawrence down at Montreal, a place Eddie had only ever seen on the map at the front of the classroom. And the St. Lawrence joined up with the Atlantic, and across the Atlantic was Scotland, where there was no lumber left, to hear his father talk. Just stones and fiddle tunes and Mama's family. Papa had no family left, to hear him talk.

A compass of some kind. Like a miniature wheel, it would fit nicely in a grown man's palm. If he were a captain out at sea, Eddie would hold this instrument suspended from a ring and, with one eye closed, sight a star along the arm. Then you could read on the circle at what angle the star was above the horizon and somehow out of all that know what the latitude was — where in the world you were.

An astrolabe: the word means star-taker. It might as well have been a star Eddie uncovered that day from its mossy bed. He had a hold of it about as long as a person might hold onto a star. A gritty star of a pleasing weight in the hand. Cool, greeny gold.

"Father," he said. "Look at this."

Eddie walked over to his father, who was standing, stretching, about to start work again. He took a deep bite on a half-eaten apple, turned the yellow compass-like thing over in his hands a couple of times, chewing thoughtfully. He nodded.

Eddie's father had been to sea, once. But if he, a boy then himself, had ventured up on deck some sleepless night and seen the captain sighting stars, it wouldn't have been with an astrolabe. A cross-staff, maybe; a quadrant more likely. No one in the 1800s used an astrolabe anymore.

Still and all, Father seemed to know or guess what he was holding, though he might not know it by name. Eddie's father might not talk much, but he knew a lot. Now he looked over to where the boy had found the thing. He looked beyond the spot through the clearing and the smoke of the fire, as if someone might come traipsing out of the woods through that smoke, eyes cast down, looking for something he'd lost.

A bluejay yelling at them from the top of a pine seemed to wake Father from a reverie. He placed the yellow circle on the stump where he had sat to eat his lunch. There would be time to look at it later. Time to shine it up, Eddie thought.

Captain Overman didn't notice it there on the stump when he came by to see how the job was progressing. But nosy old Captain Cowley had ridden down to the site with Overman, and he sniffed about while the other men discussed the business at hand. He hurled a stone at the heron to watch it fly off. He laughed, nudged Eddie in the ribs trying to get him to laugh, too. Eddie moved out of his way, busied himself with some trifle of the oxen's tracings, tucking his head back along his neck like the heron in flight.

Then, suddenly, he heard Cowley exclaim, "Wo ho! What's this, then?"

Maybe a little bit of the brass surface had come clean in the boy's handling of it. Maybe the traitorous sunlight gave the discovery away.

"Wo ho!"

Cowley was what Eddie's mama called a "boisterous lot."

"Whadya say, boy?" he said, grinning at Eddie in a way that made him angry, as if he had been trying to hide the blasted thing. If only.

Overman came right away. They both knew what the thing was, though neither of them said as much. Eddie could see something pass between them, something secret and exclusive.

"Well, I never," said Overman.

"Ever handled one of these before?" said Cowley. He wanted to take it back from Overman, but Overman held it out of the shorter man's reach. It was at that precise moment, as the young captain kept the item away from the grasping, old captain —it was at that moment that Eddie lost it for good.

"It's the boy's," said Eddie's father.

"I'll give him ten dollars for it," said Overman, ignoring Eddie. Eddie stood there, his fingers itching. Ten dollars.

"It ain't for sale," Eddie wanted to say. But *ten dollars*. Three days of a grown man's wages ...

Eddie shrugged — and this is the important thing about it—it wasn't a yes, just a shrug!

How had the thing got there? How long had it lain in the earth? What made it worth so much? The questions crowded the boy's thinking. His tongue felt bee-stung and useless. But would anything he had to say have made a difference?

I would have hidden it in the biscuit tin, you're saying to yourself. Perhaps. Or maybe you would have spoken up, brashly. "Excuse me, Captain, sir, but I'd like to think about this." Sure, you'd have said something like that! But Eddie was less than hired labour to the likes of Captain Overman.

Why didn't his father say something? Didn't he see how uncomfortable Eddie was? Hell, the captain talked to Eddie's father as if he were little more than a slave—Eddie, he paid no attention to at all.

And so the boy watched as the captain slipped the thing in his saddlebag, mounted his horse and, with a tip of his cap, rode off, with Cowley alongside scowling a bit at his own loss. Eddie watched the men ride away long after they had disappeared from view. For the rest of his life Captain Overman would ride away from that clearing with Eddie's discovery tucked in his saddlebag.

━━━

Mama had enough words for two parents when she heard what had happened. Father just went out to do the animals.

"If you'd just got it home," she shouted, loud enough that the words followed him out to the pigs. "If you'd just got the blessed item home!" She made it sound like a relic, like something sacred up at the Roman Church. Something that might have been dropped by Christ in his travels, perhaps. She didn't know what it was Overman had gotten away with. She only knew he'd gotten away with something. An injustice had been done. "He'd 'ave had his hands full trying to get the cursed item out from under my nose," she called after Father. And now the item sounded like something belonging to the Devil. Eddie only hugged little Isabel and pondered these things in his heart.

That's how it happened. How long did he hold it? A handful of minutes.

Time passed. The job at Green Lake ended. Overman paid off Eddie's father for his work but nothing was said about the blessed and cursed item. Father gave Eddie a three-dollar bill. But Eddie never saw a penny for his find, not so much as a farthing.

Many years later he would read a story in the *Renfrew Journal* (the paper in those days, before the *Mercury* came along). Eddie was a man by then, but the whole business came flooding back to him. It was his discovery they were talking about in the article, though his name figured nowhere. An astrolabe, it was. Now the item had a name, at last, though Eddie would always tend to call it "the item," remembering his mama's fire on that August day. Then another name jumped off the page of the newspaper and slapped Eddie — a full-grown man, remember — across both cheeks.

He read, "Evidence points strongly to the instrument being one lost by Samuel de Champlain."

Eddie's eyes blurred, the words disconnected like birds let out of a cage and flying up into his face. He blinked. He read again. He had attained only a modest education, Edward George Lee, but he knew well enough who Champlain was. The Father of French Canada; one of the greatest explorers of the Age of Exploration.

But even a great explorer, it seems, makes mistakes. Led to believe there was a quick route to the North Sea up the Ottawa River, Champlain took an expedition that way in 1613. He kept an extensive diary, including regular readings of his astrolabe to determine his latitude. He was a mapmaker, after all. And there was, before him, an uncharted country — uncharted in the ways of the Europeans, that is.

Champlain doesn't mention losing his astrolabe in those diaries, but there is a point at which, all of a sudden, instead of giving an exact reading of 45° 34', for instance, he says, "We are now at somewhere around 47." *And this point is where Eddie found the astrolabe.*

According to the great explorer's diary, the little expedition ran into what foresters call a windfall. It was hard slogging through thick pine growth blown down by a tornado. In Eddie's mind's eye he could see it: these men clambering over great logs, through slashing thorns and the mud of late spring. He knew just how impenetrable such a stretch of forest could be; how easy it would be for something to fall from your pack, your pocket . . .

"The astrolabe was unearthed by a fourteen-year-old boy near Cobden," said the article. It was a quote from Captain Overman, now retired. The captain went on to say what a crying shame it was that the Canadian government could not see its way clear to purchase this extraordinary relic of Canadian history for the people of this great dominion.

The asking price was only five hundred dollars.

Overman, a local man, as he was described by the *Renfrew Journal*, was credited with finding the priceless artifact. That's what the article said. An unnamed boy unearthed it; the captain found it. The eight years of schooling Edward George Lee had had were not quite enough to understand the difference between "unearthing" and "finding" something. He would never really figure that out. But as his mama would have said, bless her soul, an injustice had been done. His heart told him as much.

To be sure, Overman no longer owned the "instrument." He had given it to his boss, R. W. Cassels, the president of the Ottawa Forwarding Company, as a present. It was Cassels who would have gained from the sale. But as Eddie read the article, it was not ten dollars or even five hundred dollars that was on his mind. In his mind's eye, he could see his father holding the beautiful filthy mystery in his hands and staring off through the smoke looking for someone who might suddenly appear: a man, his eyes cast down, looking for something he had lost.

———

Champlain's astrolabe has gone through many hands since Edward George Lee held it briefly on that bright August morning, but it now belongs to the people of Canada. In 1989 the Canadian government bought the relic from an American antique collector and put it on display in the Museum of Civilization in Hull, Quebec. And on the card below it is also a passing mention of the nameless fourteen-year-old boy who discovered it. Famous and forgotten.

How I would like to have held that thing in my hands. How I would have liked to clean it up, with baby Isabel sitting nearby watching as the shine came through. I would have glinted the light from the oil lamp into her eyes off the shiny side of Champlain's astrolabe and made her laugh. How wonderful it would have been to take the item apart and ream out two hundred years of grit, make it so the arm turned smoothly, the thing could work again. How I would have liked to hold it up on a cool August night and sight along that arm, measure some star's angle above the horizon and know, if only for a moment, where in the world I was.

Scientists say that at the beginning of time there was a Big Bang, and that *everything* in the universe was created in that holy explosion. So we are stardust. Imagine that. Everything stardust. Stars in our own right.

I wonder what Edward George Lee would have had to say about that?

Based on a true account by Charles MacNamara in *The Canadian Field-Naturalist*, December, 1919.